LIGHTHOUSE COVE

RACHEL HANNA

FOREWORD

Thank you for reading the South Carolina Sunsets series! This is book 7, but you will find a link to the next book in the back of this one. Hope you enjoy Lighthouse Cove!

CHAPTER 1

*D*ixie stepped back and looked at her masterpiece. "Well, this is just about the best book display I've ever seen, don't you think?" She proudly held out her arms and looked at Julie, who was thumbing through the latest gardening magazine they'd gotten in at the store.

"It's a sight to behold," she said, laughing. Julie walked over and picked up one of the books. "Who is this author, anyway?"

"Charlotte McLemore. Haven't you heard of her? She's the biggest thing since my hair in the nineties!" Dixie cackled at her own joke, slapping her leg which was adorned with a pair of bright pink capri pants.

Spring had sprung, and that meant Dixie's clothing would get more flamboyant by the day. She loved hot weather, not that it ever got overly cold in the lowcountry. At nighttime, it dipped down into the thirties at times, but daytime temps in winter were usually in the sixties. Still, Dixie didn't break out her craziest clothing until the temperatures warmed up substantially.

"I haven't heard of her, but then I've been focused on helping Meg plan the wedding. I didn't realize how much work it would be!"

"Can I help you do anything?"

Julie waved her hand. "Nope. Not a thing. You're busy enough working here and taking care of your husband. How's he doing, by the way?"

Harry had wrenched his back trying to dig a garden in their backyard. "Oh, he'll be fine. Doc says he just needs to take it easy and stop acting like he's twenty-five again."

Julie smiled. "Is that what I have to look forward to with Dawson in a few years?"

Dixie sat down on the high stool she had placed near her. "Oh, sugar, they get worse as they get older. Always trying to do things that they should hire someone else to do. And Harry is just as stubborn as a mule!"

"Um, I think you might be similar in that regard."

Dixie laughed. "Yes, but I *can* do everything!"

The truth was, Dixie had Parkinson's disease. While she was getting on fine so far thanks to great medications and physical therapy, there was always the reality looming that she and Harry would start to progress more quickly and be unable to care for themselves. It was something Julie thought about a lot, and she'd even spoken to William about it once or twice. Each and every one of them watched Dixie like a hawk, looking for any signs that she wasn't doing well. So far, though, she was still as spry as ever.

"Knock, knock," SuAnn said as she walked into the bookstore. Even though the door chimed, Julie's mother insisted on saying knock knock every time she came into the store.

"Hey, Mom," Julie said, waving from the back wall.

"What are y'all doing back here?"

"Setting up a new Charlotte McLemore display," Dixie said.

"Oh, I love her books! Have you read her latest one with the magnolia flower on the cover?" SuAnn asked, excited. Julie had never known her mother to be a reader.

"Since when do you read?"

"Oh, dear, you can't help it if you ever read one of her books. She will draw you right in with her emotional stories, and they all have a little mystery too."

"They really are good, Julie. You should read one," Dixie said, reaching over to hand her a book.

Julie laughed and held up her hand. "Do y'all understand that I'm planning a wedding, running

3

an inn, working here, raising a new son and helping to plan Meg's wedding? I have no time to read!"

Dixie nodded. "You're right. There is a lot on your plate. Why don't you let us help you? I can make phone calls or watch Dylan…"

Julie rubbed her arm. "Thank you. And I may take you up on that soon."

"And seeing as how I am Meg's grandmother, it would be nice if you'd let me help with something too," SuAnn said, her voice giving Julie the distinct impression that she was feeling left out.

"I wanted to talk to you about that. Meg wants to have a dessert bar instead of a big cake. She wondered if you'd make a variety of desserts?"

"Of course. I'll work on a menu."

"Thanks. So, what's going on with you today?"

"Well, I came to tell you the latest gossip."

"Oh, do tell," Julie said, pretending to be overly interested. Actually, she was a little curious.

"Well, Darcy heard from her friend Avery that there's a new lighthouse keeper."

"Lighthouse keeper? That place has been closed down for years," Dixie said.

"Well, apparently the county has restored it, and they hired someone to live in that little house next to it. They're going to be starting tours and opening a little gift shop. Whoever this mystery person is will be running all of that."

"That's great! Anything that brings more tourists," Julie said.

"Well, I just hope the person is decent and not some troublemaker who will wreak havoc in our beloved town," SuAnn said.

Julie rolled her eyes. "Oh, yes, let's not have any troublemakers move here, Mom."

SuAnn tossed a magazine at her as they all laughed.

~

A s she stood there, staring up at the tall black and white lighthouse, she wondered if she was up to this task. The last few months had taken a toll on her in a way she couldn't really describe in words, and it wasn't often that her words failed her.

She stepped out of her small, compact car and shut the door. Surprisingly, it had gotten her here all the way from Nashville, although there was that moment near Knoxville where she thought the wheel might pop off. Thankfully, it turned out to be a pothole in the road, but it sure gave her quite a shock.

Emma Mackenzie had spent her life taking care of people, first her sick mother and then her dysfunctional grandmother. Now, she was responsible for this huge lighthouse, and it would be impossible to hide her imperfections when she was the one guiding strangers through the tall building day after day.

Sure, she could've said no to this job, but when her old friend had told her about it, she'd been intrigued. After all, her previous line of work was nothing like this. Every day had been stressful and full of adrenaline. Surely, walking people through a lighthouse would be a cakewalk compared to that.

Never mind that she knew next to nothing about lighthouses, except what she'd learned watching YouTube videos and grilling her old friend. Paul had been a buddy of hers in high school, and when he'd heard about her recent situation, he'd been the first to step up with the opportunity. He lived in Atlanta now, working as a headhunter mostly for the tech industry, but he had connections in Seagrove and one thing had led to another.

After meetings with the county, mostly virtual, she'd been hired. A part of her was scared a bit, but the larger part of her was grateful to get away from regular life. Escaping to a small island that nobody had even heard of made her feel safer than she had in years.

When she looked at the ocean, it reminded her of her mother. She'd passed away almost ten years ago now, but Emma would've given anything to have one more day with her. She so loved the ocean. They went on beach vacations a lot when she was a kid, even though her mother was working two jobs just to pay for things like that. Having never had a father in her life, Emma had counted on her mom. Although she'd been in her late twenties when her mom was diagnosed with stage four brain cancer, it hadn't made it any easier. She needed her, even now, at forty years old.

She had especially needed her when she had to step up and take care of her grandmother. The woman had been impossible to deal with for most of her life, and being responsible for her after her own mother had passed away almost destroyed her. In the end, a stroke in her sleep had taken her, but not before she'd taken just about everything out of Emma. That was already a year ago. How time flew.

"Oh good! You made it!"

A woman walked toward her, a smile on her face. She looked overly made up for the area, and her hair was so high that it looked like cotton candy piled on her head.

"Yes. Sorry I'm a little late. There was traffic coming through Charleston."

She waved her hand. "No problem. We don't really follow time too closely around here. I'm Henrietta. We spoke on the phone?"

Emma nodded. "Oh, yes. Nice to meet you."

"Why don't you follow me, and I'll show you to your new home."

Before Emma could respond, Henrietta was high-tailing it down the gravel driveway toward a small cottage. She quickly followed behind her, a trail of small pebbles popping up under Henrietta's chunky high-heels.

The cottage was nice enough from the outside. It was brick painted white and mainly just a little square building. Nothing fancy, but that was okay. The simpler the better as far as Emma was concerned. Her life had been far too complicated for too long. She needed air and space and calmness.

Henrietta keyed the door and opened it, standing back so Emma could walk inside first. She was surprised at just how nice it was. They had obviously redecorated the place recently as it had a farmhouse look to it with whitewashed walls and distressed wood floors. Emma was pleasantly surprised.

"It's very cute."

"Isn't it? Just adorable. Now, there's one bedroom, one bathroom, living room and kitchen. All the basics."

"Great."

"The kitchen has been stocked with pots and pans and so forth. We did a small grocery run just so you'd have some stuff here. Milk, eggs, those kinds of things."

"Sounds like you thought of everything."

"We try. Well, here's your keys." She handed Emma a small keyring, her big pink nails almost scratching Emma's finger. "Now, Roger will contact you tomorrow about doing a lighthouse walk-through. We have a whole script you can use for the tours, and those won't start for another week or so."

"Got it."

"Better run. I'm meeting my friend, SuAnn for lunch. She owns the bakery over the bridge. You might want to try it some time. The best poundcake you've ever put in your mouth!"

Emma forced a smile. She was too tired to care about poundcake right now. "I'll keep that in mind."

As she watched Henrietta drive away, she wondered if she'd made the right decision coming to Seagrove. The town seemed nice enough, but was she ready to finally look at her life and deal with everything that had happened in the last year?

"I don't understand this…" Dylan groaned as he stared at his math worksheet, He laid his forehead on the paper and sighed. "Can't I just quit school and work for you?"

Dawson chuckled. Although he did need help around the inn, it probably wasn't the best idea to let his nine-year-old son quit school. "No, buddy. You need to finish school so you can become something important like a doctor."

Dylan looked at him. "I don't want to be a doctor."

"What do you want to be then?"

"I want to be a race car driver and a chef."

Dawson smiled. "You can do anything you want to do, Dylan. But first, you have to master third grade math."

Dylan sighed. "Can I take a break?"

He'd been at it for over an hour, so Dawson agreed. "Sure. Why don't you go help Lucy fix dinner? I'm sure she could use the help."

Without missing a beat, Dylan trotted off to the kitchen. Dawson loved being a dad. Dylan was everything he'd ever wanted in a son, and each day with him was like learning something new. Watching him take in the world around him, discover new things and experience so much joy made Dawson feel so happy.

"Where's the kiddo?" Julie asked as she walked into the dining room. She'd been working long hours lately, trying to manage the bookstore and planning Meg's wedding. Each time he'd offered help, she'd declined, not wanting to put anybody out. That was his wife. She tried to do it all, and eventually she'd realize she couldn't. He was just waiting for that moment so he could swoop in and help her. It was their pattern, and he'd grown to expect it and love it.

Dawson hugged her and kissed the top of her head. "Math overcame him, so he's helping Lucy with dinner."

Julie laughed. "Math does that to me too."

"Ditto."

She looked up at him. "And how is my handsome husband this evening?"

"He was missing his wife, but he's all good now."

"Good. What's for dinner?" she asked as she walked over to the chair and sat down, dropping her purse strap over the back of it.

"Lucy said we're having meatloaf, mashed potatoes and salad tonight."

"Yum. That should hit the spot after a long day."

"Was the store busy?"

"Getting busier now that tourists are arriving. Spring has officially sprung."

"Yeah, bookings are up too. We got three new ones today alone. Of course, those aren't coming until June."

She smiled, tiredly. "I'm glad people are booking, though. Gotta keep this place full."

He nodded. "True."

"Mommy!" Dylan said, running out of the kitchen. He wrapped his arms around her neck and hugged her. Dawson loved watching their interactions. Even when Julie was tired, she always had energy for their son. It was often hard to imagine what life was like before he was a father. These moments, small and often lost on others, meant the world to him after losing his first child. He thought he'd lost his opportunity to be a dad, but then God had stepped up and given him something more amazing than he'd ever expected - a family of his own.

"Hey, buddy! How was school today?"

Dylan grumbled. "Third grade is impossible, Mom."

She looked up at Dawson, stifling a laugh. "Is that so?"

He stood up and sat in the chair next to her. "We had three math worksheets for homework tonight. Can you believe that?"

"Wow. That's a lot of work, but I know you're so smart that you'll knock that right out."

He looked at her for a moment. "I guess so."

"And I told him if he finishes, he gets cherry cobbler after dinner," Lucy said, breezing into the dining room with a bowl of mashed potatoes in one hand and a pitcher of gravy in the other. If there was one thing Lucy could make well, it was her home-made gravy. Dawson had loved it for years, and he'd asked her for the recipe many times. She always said that it was her job security and she'd only leave to him in her will.

"Yum… cherry cobbler…." Dylan said, rubbing his stomach. Dawson often looked at his energetic son and wondered what his life had really been like before they adopted him. What had he seen? What had he experienced? He couldn't think about it for long without his blood pressure rising and his eyes filling with tears.

Lucy brought the rest of the food to the table as everyone got settled into their chairs. This was Dawson's favorite time of day, when his family was all there together.

"So, how was the bookstore today?" Dawson asked.

"It was busy. Dixie was very excited about this author's books and set up a big display. Almost takes up the whole front entrance," Julie said with a laugh.

"Which author?" Lucy asked as she placed a cloth napkin in her lap.

"Charlotte McLemore."

Lucy smiled and clapped her hands. "Oh, she's my favorite! Her books have so much emotion that you end up staying awake all night to read them!"

"That's what I hear."

"So, what else?"

"Mom came to the store today," Julie said as she took a sip of her tea.

"Uh oh. What's my mother-in-law up to now?" Dawson asked, smiling. SuAnn was a loose cannon, for sure. Sometimes she was as sweet as sugar, but she could cut you really quickly with her words and actions. He found it was best to stay in her good graces and keep himself out of the line of fire if he could. So far, that had worked well.

"She needed to tell us the latest gossip that we have a new resident in town who will be running the lighthouse now that renovations are complete. There will be tours and everything."

Dawson had been in the lighthouse many times having grown up on the island. It sat at the tip of the island and had long since been out of commission, but seeing it repaired and working again was a good thing in his mind. Still, any time someone new moved to their little paradise, everyone worried. Would the person be a problem? Would they get along with everyone? Would they be a contributing member of the community or take away from the culture there?

"Do we know who it is?"

"Nope. My detective of a mother had shockingly little information. I'm sure she'll dig something up soon like the bloodhound that she is," Julie said, laughing as she scooped up a spoonful of mashed potatoes.

"Oh, you can bet on that."

CHAPTER 2

*E*mma stood at the bottom of the lighthouse circular staircase and looked up to the top. She was in good shape, especially considering her former job, but nothing had prepared her for this.

As she looked at Roger, the man tasked with training her on all things lighthouse related, she wondered how he'd drag his chubby frame up the steps. What if she had to do mouth-to-mouth on him at the top? That would certainly be a terrible introduction to her new job.

Roger took a handkerchief out of his pocket and wiped his already sweaty forehead. It wasn't that hot outside, but she was sure after their walk up the gazillion stairs, he was going to need a towel.

They started to walk up the stairs as Roger rattled on about the history of the structure. She knew she had to listen, but she was distracted by so many unrelated thoughts ping-ponging around her head. During her first night in the cottage, she'd gotten an unexpected phone call, and she was desperately trying not to think about it.

"The lighthouse was constructed in eighteen-hundred and twenty-seven, but it was renovated after the Civil War due to damage it suffered. Now, there was also some damage in eighteen-hundred and eighty-six after the Charleston earthquake…"

Did she need to know all of these details, she wondered. Were tourists really coming to learn dates and history or were they just wanting a good workout and a nice view at the top? A place to take a picture they could post on social media to pretend their lives were perfect so that a bunch of strangers would be jealous of them? She hoped the latter and feared the former.

"We've had our share of hurricanes over the years which required some minor repairs along the way…" he said as he struggled up the last of the stairs. She held up her hands for a moment, thinking he might fall backward and crush her. Roger had to be in his sixties, and maybe even older, but she had to give it to him. He knew his history and he made it to the top.

"Now, how much do you know about the lenses on lighthouses?" he asked, leaning against the wall for support.

She stared at him like a deer caught in headlights. "Um… I watched a video on YouTube."

He stared at her for a moment. "What's YouTube?"

Again, she froze in place, unsure if he was joking or just sadly out of touch with modern life. Finally, he let out a big, hearty laugh and slapped her shoulder. "I'm just messing with you, Emma. I know what YouTube is. I even have a channel."

"*You* have a channel?" she said, a little amazed.

"Sure! Doesn't everybody? I like to talk about fishing in the lowcountry. I'll give you the name of the channel in a minute so you can check it out."

She was never going to check it out.

"This here is what you call a Fresnel lens. The way that it's cut allows light…"

As he continued talking, she got the very smart idea of recording him on her phone so she could study it later. Plus, she didn't have to pay attention right now while her mind was wandering around like a highly-caffeinated squirrel.

When her estranged boyfriend had called her last night, it had been very unexpected. After all, he was one of the things she was running away from. Not that he was abusive or anything, but he was a part of her old life that she was desperate to leave behind. Nobody understood, but she knew what was best for her, and she was determined to start over. What better place to do that than an isolated lowcountry island?

"Our marshes have over two-hundred species of birds…"

What on Earth was he talking about now? Birds? How was that related to the lighthouse? She'd definitely have to re-watch the video she was taking to understand the correlation there. Right now, she wanted to stand at the top of the lighthouse and stare out over the water while she pondered how her life had gone off the rails.

Just a few months ago, she was where she thought she should be. Working in her chosen career field and operating at the top of her game. Or so she thought. Until *that* day. The one day that would change everything. How she wished she could go back and change things. But sometimes things rip through your life in a way that can never be stitched back together.

"What are you watching?" Tucker asked as he walked up behind Colleen. She was sitting at her desk, supposedly working on plans for the next holiday season, but her mind needed a break. Thankfully, she and Tucker were alone in the office, so she could take a few minutes to unwind if she wanted.

"What do you think?" she asked with a laugh. It had become well known to Tucker that Colleen was obsessed with true crime and mystery videos. She watched them all the time, and she loved trying to solve them. Sometimes, she wondered if she should've been a detective or something.

"How do you watch that stuff so much?" He leaned over and kissed her cheek before handing her a bottle of water. Tucker was always bugging her to drink more water.

"I love trying to solve mysteries."

"Well, maybe you can solve this one," he said, holding up a file folder.

"What?"

"Where'd the drawings go for the robot dog I was working on?"

Colleen laughed. "I transferred them to the tablet. Honestly, Tucker, I don't know anyone our age who still uses paper to sketch things. You have this expensive program you're supposed to be using." She held up the tablet.

Tucker shook his head. "I like the feel of paper when I draw."

Colleen got up and hugged him. "I know, honey. You're an old man trapped in a young body. But, you're my old man."

"Yuck, stop all that lovey-dovey stuff," Meg said as she walked into the office with Vivi on her hip. She handed her to Colleen like she was a bomb about to go off. "Here, take your niece. She's being a handful today!"

Colleen laughed. "No, that can't be right. My Vivi is a perfect angel." She pressed a big kiss onto Vivi's cheek as her niece kicked and bucked like a wild mule.

"She wants to run around all over the place, so holding her is impossible right now," Meg said, falling into one of the rolling office chairs nearby. "I saw y'all through the window and decided to thrust my problem child upon you for a few minutes."

"Where are you headed?" Colleen asked as she sat down with Vivi on her lap. Within seconds, she was plundering though everything on the top of Colleen's desk. The empty stapler seemed to be her favorite.

"I went by the bakery so grandma could see Vivi, and then I stopped by the bookstore to get her some learning cards. We're starting to teach her to read."

Colleen stared at her. "Isn't she a little young to be reading?

"Actually, this is a great age to start teaching her to read," Tucker interjected. "Studies show…"

"Never mind, Mr. Know-It-All," Colleen said with a laugh as she pried her most important file out of Vivi's hands. She gave her a little stuffed teddy bear to play with, until she got bored with it, of course.

"Did y'all hear the latest news?" Meg asked.

"No, what?"

"Well, it seems we have a new resident here. Grandma told me all about it. Some woman moved here to take care of the lighthouse."

"I thought that place was closed down?" Tucker said.

"Not anymore. They fixed it up and will be giving tours."

"I'm glad to hear it. The lighthouse is such a big part of Seagrove. Can't wait to see the view from up there," Colleen said. "Maybe a date night in the near future?"

Tucker smiled. "Anything you want, dear."

"Even though you're afraid of heights?" she said, smiling up at him.

"I'm not exactly afraid. I just prefer the ground."

"Uh huh," she mumbled as she tickled Vivi in an effort to distract her. Letting her run around the office would be a disaster. They worked in the toy industry, after all. She'd break every prototype they were working on.

"Well, I better get home. Christian is coming home early so we can chill out and watch a movie tonight as a family."

"Sounds fun," Colleen said, standing up and handing Vivi back to her sister.

"The reality is that we'll probably fall asleep before it's halfway over. This wedding planning is exhausting!"

"Oh, that reminds me. I tried on the maid of honor dress, and it just needed some hemming. Otherwise, we're good to go on that. We still need to meet at the florist one day soon, though."

"Right. I'll add that to my ever-growing list," she said, typing it into her phone. "See y'all later!"

As Colleen watched her little sister disappear down the sidewalk, she couldn't help but be proud of her. Having a child so young couldn't be easy, and she admired how she'd handled it. She was a great mother, and she was going to be an amazing wife too.

E mma stood at the top of the lighthouse. She stared off into the ocean, her thoughts a mixture of gratitude and sadness. Disappointment in herself and hope for a better future. It was quite a dichotomy.

Her grandmother, for all the trouble she'd caused in her life, had given her a good piece of advice once. "Emma," she'd said, "Life is going to throw rocks at you one day. At first, they're going to nail you right in that pretty face of yours. You'll have scars and pain from it, but next time you'll know to put your hands up. Because, after all, nobody wants life to beat them up and make them look ugly for the rest of their days. When life throws rocks, for goodness sakes, put your hands up and fight."

Moving to Seagrove was her way of fighting. Maybe others would consider it running away, just like her boyfriend did. But, for her it meant preserving her sanity. Giving her room to breathe again. Getting out of the spotlight that she'd found herself in unwillingly.

She watched a bird fly overhead, and a feeling of loneliness washed over her. She knew no one on this island, apart from Henrietta and Roger. And, unless she wanted to join the local senior center, she doubted those two people would be her new best friends.

A part of her wanted to find new friends. She was only forty years old, after all. She wasn't retired. She needed interaction. But the other larger part of her said no. She didn't need anyone who would ask questions or judge her. She'd had quite enough of that.

Just as she was about to make her way down the stairs and into the cottage for an early dinner, her phone vibrated in her pocket. She usually didn't answer it, but she couldn't say no when it was her only real friend, Caroline.

They'd met when they were in kindergarten, and the only person who'd really been there for her over the last year was Caroline. From burying her grandmother, to the day she wanted to forget, her friend had tried so hard to be her rock. "Hello?"

"Emma? Thank goodness! I've been worried sick about you! Where on earth are you? Steve said you took your things and left?"

"That's right."

Caroline paused a moment, like she was unsure of what to say. "Honey, are you okay? Tell me where you are so I can come to you."

"I… can't."

"What do you mean? Is somebody holding you?"

Emma chuckled. "No. I just need some time."

"I understand, but you shouldn't be alone, Em. I'll come, and I won't tell a soul. I promise."

A tear welled in her eye. "I know you would come, but I just want to do this alone, okay?"

"Emma, I have to ask this question…"

"What question?"

"Are you… a danger to yourself?"

"No! I promise I'm not. In fact, my head is starting to feel clearer already."

"Are you sure? I can get you whatever help you need. You know that." Caroline was a licensed clinical social worker, and her skills had helped Emma after the "incident". But there were still dark corners of her soul that no amount of counseling was going to touch. Her hope was that the ocean would wash them away.

"I'm sure. Look, I'm going to be okay. I just

needed to get away from all of it. I know Steve doesn't understand, but I need you to make him leave me alone. Okay?"

"He loves you, Em."

"If he loved me, he would stop trying to contact me. He needs to move on, Caroline. It's what's best. We're never getting back together."

Caroline cleared her throat. "Okay. I'll try to talk to him."

"Thanks. Listen, I've got some things to do. I'll touch base soon, okay?"

"Okay. I love you, Em." She could hear Caroline's voice shaking a bit.

"I love you too."

As she pressed end, she looked up at the bird that had been flying overhead. Now, a flock had joined it and they formed a V before flying off. It hadn't been alone, after all. It had been looking for its flock, and they hadn't let it down. She hoped to find her own flock one day. For now, she'd be that lone bird, aimlessly zipping around in the sky, waiting for some kind of direction.

Janine stood in the kitchen, looking out over the marsh behind the cabin. From the moment she'd moved in, this had felt like her happy place. She loved the abundant wildlife she saw each day, from birds to the occasional alligator. The smell of the marsh was hard to describe, and it had grown on her. Of course, mosquito repellant had become more required than fancy perfume, not that she normally wore that either.

She lifted her coffee cup to her lips, savoring the warmth as it passed from her throat to her stomach. Being petite meant always being cold, even in the often muggy lowcountry.

"I'm off to work! See you tonight!" Colleen called as she hurried toward the front door.

"Have a good day!" Janine yelled back, as she always did.

Having her niece as her roommate had been a godsend. Their relationship had grown, after years of not seeing each other when she and Julie had been estranged. Now, surrounded by more family than ever, Janine finally felt at home.

Of course, having a wonderful boyfriend like William helped too. Seagrove felt like the place she was always meant to be, and she didn't see herself ever leaving. She finally understood what people meant when they said they had put down roots.

"Knock, knock," Julie said, poking her head in the front door.

"Oh, hey, sis. What a surprise to see you so early this morning. Everything okay?" she asked as she walked into the living room.

"Yeah, everything is great. Just thought I'd stop by

26

before work and see how you've been doing. I feel like I never get to talk to you anymore between work and planning the wedding."

Janine sat on the sofa and patted the seat next to her. "Come sit."

"Are you all right?" Julie asked as she put her purse on the back of the chair and sat on the sofa.

"Of course! Just enjoying some coffee before my first classes. You want a cup?"

"No thanks. I had some of Dawson's coffee this morning."

Janine chuckled. "That'll put hair on your chest."

"Definitely. I swear his coffee is thicker than tar!"

Janine had missed these times with her sister, especially mornings. When they were living together before Julie married Dawson, they were like teenagers again. Late night talks, early morning walks. Coffee, chips and the occasional cupcake. Now, it seemed like they were growing apart. Julie was a new mother again, and Janine had no kids. Julie had a business, a husband and a granddaughter. Her life was full, and Janine was starting to feel like hers wasn't.

"How's Dylan?"

Julie laughed. "He's a handful, as usual. Dawson signed him up for karate to work off some of that excess energy and teach him discipline."

"Oh, that's great!"

"Yeah, he starts next week. But he's a great kid."

"He is. Y'all are really blessed," Janine said, taking another sip of her coffee, trying not to make eye contact.

"Okay, what's going on?"

"What do you mean?"

"Sis, I know when something's bothering you, and something is definitely bothering you. What is it?"

Janine sighed and put her mug on the table in front of her. "It's no big deal, really."

"You look sad, and that's a big deal to me."

"I just feel a bit… empty lately."

"Empty? But you have the yoga studio and William. Wait, is everything okay with William?"

She nodded her head. "Yes. Better than ever. And his charter business is going really well."

"Then why do you feel empty?"

"I hate saying this because I don't want to make you feel bad…"

"Did I do something wrong?"

Janine's eyes widened. "Oh no! Not at all. It's just me. I'm a little envious, that's all."

"Envious?"

"You have it all, Julie. A marriage, a new son, a granddaughter, a business. I guess I just wish my time would come to start my own family."

Julie rubbed her arm. "Your time is coming, Janine. I just know it."

"I mean, I'm too old to have a child biologically.

That ship has sailed for me. But, I'd love to adopt like you did. I think I could provide a great home."

"You absolutely could!"

"I just don't want to do it alone."

"You want to get married?"

She nodded. "I'd love to marry William, but he seems so hesitant. Maybe he's not sure I'm the one for him. I just wish I knew for sure because I need to keep moving forward."

Before they could continue their conversation, SuAnn opened the door holding a large covered cake plate. "Morning, girls!"

"Mom, you scared me to death!" Janine said, holding her hand over her heart.

"Get dressed, Janine. We've got an errand to run, the three of us."

"I have work, Mom," Julie said, standing up.

"Oh, poo! Dixie can handle it for another half hour or so."

"Where are we going?" Janine asked.

"What kind of neighbors would we be if we didn't welcome our newest resident over at the lighthouse?"

Janine looked at her sister, each giving a knowing glance at the other. They knew what their mother was up to. She wanted the gossip, and she was ready to go straight to the source. God help the new resident because SuAnn was going to find out her life story as soon as possible.

CHAPTER 3

*E*mma knelt in the middle of the flower bed, hunched over as she pulled out weed after weed. It was amazing any flowers were growing at all, but daffodils were hearty plants, apparently. When Henrietta had called to say that the flower beds needed to look perfect before they started giving tours, Emma realized just how much she'd taken on. Was it going to be worth it just to hide from her old life?

Plus, she'd never been much of a gardener. Living in apartments for her whole adult life didn't lend itself well to getting in the dirt. Her job had been far too demanding to worry about planting flowers. Most of the time, she was working overnight hours and wouldn't see the fruits of her labor if she had planted a garden.

As she stood over the plant bed, catching her

breath, she felt a small sense of accomplishment when she looked at the pile of weeds she'd pulled. Each one represented a cleaning out of sorts, although she wasn't prone to deep metaphorical thoughts.

"Well, hello there, new neighbor!"

Emma turned to see three women standing there. The one who spoke was older, and she was carrying a large glass cake plate with something inside. The other two women, one with shoulder length straight hair and the other with a huge head of curly hair, stood there like they were embarrassed.

"Hi," Emma said. She felt a bit like the new kid at school.

"Sorry if we scared you," the straight haired woman said. She figured she should learn their names.

"Oh, it's fine. I was just working on this flower bed. I'm Emma," she said, reaching out her hand.

"Nice to meet you. I'm SuAnn, and these are my daughters, Julie and Janine."

After all of the handshakes, Emma stepped back and forced a smile. An awkward silence hung in the air for a long moment before SuAnn took over again. She was a forceful one, that was for sure.

"I own the bakery in town, so I brought you one of my famous pound cakes as a welcome to the island." SuAnn handed her the domed cake plate.

"Thank you. It'll take me awhile to finish it." The

cake was huge, and Emma was never going to be able to finish it, but she appreciated the effort anyway.

"Well, we're already here. What do you say we come in and have a piece together? We'd love to get to know you!"

Oh dear God. She wanted to come inside? The cottage was a wreck, and she wasn't really up for company right now.

"Mom, let's not intrude," Janine said, elbowing her mother.

"No, it's fine. Really. But I have to warn you that I'm still unpacking, so the house is a bit of a mess," Emma said, wishing she was brave enough to tell this woman no.

"Oh, we totally understand!" SuAnn said, smiling expectantly.

Emma turned and walked toward the front door, the three women trailing behind her. Gosh, she hoped her underwear wasn't on the top of her laundry pile in the living room.

As they walked inside, she hurried over to the living room and cleared the sofas. "Please, have a seat. I'll get us some plates."

SuAnn nodded as they all sat down on the sofa. Emma dug through the cabinets in the kitchen, trying to remember where the plates were. She still hadn't gotten the hang of the place yet. Finally, she found some small salad plates. She quickly cut four pieces of the moist poundcake and put them on the plates, grabbing some plastic forks she'd bought before returning to the living room.

"Sorry about the plastic ware. The kitchen wasn't exactly stocked when I got here. I just haven't had time to go shopping yet."

"I'll bet. It must be a huge undertaking to get this place ready for visitors," Julie said, smiling. She seemed nice. Her mother, on the other hand, seemed a bit... much. But she made a great poundcake.

"We start doing tours next week, so I'm in a bit of a time crunch."

"Hen was certainly behind the eight ball with this one," SuAnn said, shaking her head.

"Hen?"

"Henrietta. You've met her, right?"

"Oh, yes. I didn't know anyone called her Hen."

"Nobody but me," SuAnn said, smiling proudly. "But I can get away with it since we're best friends."

Noted. Don't say anything bad about Hen around SuAnn.

"Is there anything we can do to help you, Emma?" Janine asked.

Emma smiled. "Thank you, but I've got it under control even if it doesn't look that way. Where do you ladies live?"

"I have an apartment in town," SuAnn interjected before taking a bite of her cake.

"We live here on the island," Julie said. "My

33

husband and I run The Inn At Seagrove, and I'm also part owner at the bookstore. Janine lives in my old cottage."

"I run the yoga studio in town," Janine said.

"Wow. Very accomplished women," Emma said.

"We believe in strong women around here," SuAnn said, setting her empty plate on the table.

"Sorry I didn't have any coffee," Emma said, suddenly feeling like a terrible host.

"No problem. We invited ourselves at a very inopportune time," Julie said, standing up. "And we aren't going to keep you from what you need to do anymore." Janine stood too, but SuAnn wasn't budging until Julie walked over and pulled on her arm. "Besides, I need to get to work and Janine has classes to teach. Come on, Mom."

"Already? We didn't get a very long visit. I wanted to know more about you, Emma."

Emma wasn't ready to share much about herself, especially her recent past. She was thankful that Julie was practically dragging her mother out of the cottage.

"She has work to do, Mom. Let's leave her to it."

SuAnn finally stood and walked toward the door. "We'll be sure to come back and take the tour next week, so we'll get plenty of time to chat then."

Janine rolled her eyes. "Let's not threaten her, Mom."

Emma loved the back-and-forth relationship that

these grown daughters seemed to have with their mother. She wished that she'd had that, even though she could tell there was some frustration and old baggage there. Her mother had never really been motherly, and her grandma had belonged in a mental ward or possibly prison. Definitely not the stuff funny sitcoms are made of.

She said her goodbyes to the women, thankful that she didn't have to reveal much about herself during the short visit. As she watched them walk away and disappear into the mossy trees, she wondered if she'd be able to keep her cover for very long, or would someone recognize her and reveal who she really was.

Dixie stood at the end of the dock and waited for her son's boat to come back. He'd taken a small group of businessmen on a tour of the marsh, but he said he'd be back in time to meet her for lunch. It was long overdue, and she was looking forward to it.

Of course, she had an ulterior motive, as mothers often did. It was hard for her to see her son making what she thought was a mistake, and she was going to try to say something about it. Whether he appreciated her uninvited input was another question altogether.

She didn't like to think of herself as a meddler, but as she'd gotten older, she'd come to accept that part of herself. Aging had given her the ability to say what she wanted and just be considered an old woman with no filter between her mouth and brain.

Sometimes, it was refreshing that no one seemed to expect as much from her anymore. Even though she knew she could contribute just as much to society as anyone else, the unfortunate side effect of aging was that people thought you were all washed up at a certain age. It wasn't true, but she tried to use that stereotype to her advantage when she could.

Finally, she saw William's boat appear around the last turn of the marsh before his dock. She smiled and waved, and he gave her the same look he did when she showed up at school to pick him up - like she was embarrassing the heck out of him.

The three businessmen stepped out of the boat, thanked William and said hello to Dixie before walking down the path. "Hey, Mom," he said, leaning in and kissing her cheek. "Been waiting long?"

"Nah, not too bad. Thankful I sprayed myself for mosquitos before I came, though."

"Yeah, you know how marsh life is. And the no-see-ums are terrible today."

Many tourists were unprepared for the little annoying and painful flying insects, but locals knew them all too well. They were also known as biting midges, and they would swarm a person without them even realizing it. So tiny that they were almost impossible to see, the person would be left with numerous painful bites. When William was a kid, he called them "flying pirahna", and that description seemed to fit quite well.

"Ready for something to eat? I'm starving!"

He nodded. "Yeah, I've been going full-force all day. Had a fishing charter early this morning, but Janine made me breakfast to-go. My stomach is empty now. Where should we eat?"

Dixie smiled. "Well, I actually made us lunch. I thought maybe we could take a little boat trip?"

William stared at her. "Mom, I've been in that boat all day."

"I haven't." Mother guilt was always effective. Truthfully, she wanted this conversation to be as private as possible, but she also wanted to finally take a ride on her son's boat.

He sighed and hung his head. "Fine. But what did you make?"

"Chicken salad sandwiches on croissants."

"With pecans or without?"

She furrowed her eyebrows. "With, of course. What kind of woman do you take me for?"

William laughed. "Good. Just wanted to make sure you weren't cutting corners."

"Never!"

He helped her onto the boat as she held onto his hand for dear life. She wasn't as spry as she used to be, and having Parkinson's had only slowed her down more. Thankfully, the medications and physical therapy helped her preserve what she had, and she tried to exercise at least three days a week since it was supposed to be the most effective treatment for the disease.

Once they got settled, William eased the boat out into the marsh, picking a pretty area with a view of open water. Dixie loved where she lived. There was so much beauty surrounding her from the grasses of the marsh to the waves of the ocean to the historical buildings lining the streets of town. She could never imagine living anywhere else.

Dixie dug the food out of her large bag and handed William his food. They sat for a few moments, each of them taking a bite of their croissant and looking out at the water. It was getting hotter outside with each passing day, and Dixie didn't relish the humidity that was coming once the summer months arrived. Most days, she tried to stay inside in the air conditioning when summer rolled around. Plus, there were a lot more tourists milling about, so when she wasn't at work, she wanted to be in her cool home.

William placed his sandwich in his lap, wiped his mouth and looked at his mother. "Okay, out with it, Mom."

"What?" Dixie said, a mouthful of chicken salad blocking her from saying much else. She widened her eyes so much that she could feel her eyebrows raise an ungodly amount. Surely, he wasn't buying her fake innocent look.

"I know you brought me out here to talk about something. What is it?"

She wiped her mouth. "Darlin', I came to eat lunch with my only son and finally take a ride in his boat. Why do you always assume the worst about me? It's very hurtful, William."

He chuckled. "I see why you flunked high school theater."

"That was because Mrs. Calhoun hated me. She was jealous of my hair. I'll believe that 'til the day I die."

"Mom." His firm tone let Dixie know she was treading on thin ice. And after all the years they didn't speak, she wasn't willing to risk upsetting him like that again. Honesty was the best policy in this situation.

"Okay, fine. Maybe I did want to talk to you about something, but I also came to see you and ride in your boat."

"Spit it out, Mom."

"Well, son, it's just that I'm worried about you... and Janine."

He looked at her, confusion on his face. "What about me and Janine? Things are going great with us."

"Are you sure, honey? I mean, are you certain that Janine feels that way?"

He put his food on the seat beside him and leaned forward. "What are you talking about?"

"It's just that women… well, some women… especially of a certain age… well, they want things… and men don't always see it for what it is…"

"Have you taken your medication today?"

"What?"

"You're stammering like you can't get your words out."

She sighed and threw her hands in the air. "Janine wants to get married! Okay? I said it. And it wasn't my place to say it!"

"Then why are you saying it?"

"Because you weren't getting any of my hints!"

They both stopped and took a deep breath. "Who told you that? Janine?"

"Of course not!"

"Then who?"

"Does it matter?"

"Yes, it matters. I need to know if it was a reputable source."

Dixie nodded her head. "Oh, honey, it was a very reputable source."

"Mom, tell me."

She hung her head. "It was Julie."

"Julie told you that Janine wants to get married?"

"No. She told Dawson. I just overheard the

conversation. She thought I'd left the shop, and she was chatting with Dawson on the phone."

"So you were eavesdropping."

"Not on purpose."

"Did you tell her you overheard the conversation?"

Dixie shook her head. "Didn't seem necessary. Look, I'm not SuAnn. I don't go around gossiping, but this seemed important enough to tell you."

He stood up and ran his fingers through his hair. "I mean, we've talked about marriage a few times, but things have just been going so well that it didn't occur to me that there was a rush or anything."

"Sweetie, what're you waiting for? I mean, far be it for me to say, but y'all aren't getting any younger."

"Thanks a lot, Mom," he said, rolling his eyes.

"William, I just want to see you happy. Life is a lot shorter than you think." Her life with Johnny, her late husband, had been so much shorter than either of them ever thought it would be.

"I love Janine. I guess I was just trying to make something of myself again before I asked her. I want to feel worthy of being her husband." Dixie's heart melted when she heard her son say that.

She leaned over and touched his arm, being careful not to stand up in the unstable boat. Parkinson's didn't exactly give her wonderful balance. The last thing she needed was to fall head first into the marsh and get eaten by some creature lurking below.

"Now, listen to your old momma," she said, putting her hand on his cheek. "You're worthy of any woman. Janine would be blessed to have you as a husband, and you would be blessed to have her as a wife. Stop overthinking things, my handsome son. Love isn't something to be thought about; it's something to be felt and cherished."

William smiled. "You should write greeting cards, Mom."

"Maybe in my next lifetime," she joked as she eased herself back down onto the small seat. "So, what're you going to do?"

He looked at her and then out over the water. "I don't know. I need some time to think, I suppose."

"Just don't think too long, William. Life just keeps moving on."

The darkness was overwhelming. She walked along the edge of the wall, her back brushing against it as she tried to look around the corner. But it was so dark. So devastatingly dark. She couldn't hear anything over the wild beating of her heart. It wasn't like she hadn't been in situations like this a million times before, but this one was different. She could feel it in her bones, like a dark foreboding that she couldn't shake no matter how hard she tried.

Her palms were sweating. The hairs on the back

of her neck stood at attention like diligent soldiers waiting on their next orders. Why did she have to be alone? She tried to quiet her breath, but it felt like her throat was constricting. What if she stopped breathing? Her heart was beating so hard and fast that she wondered if a heart could actually explode. She didn't want to find out.

She inched closer and closer to the corner. Why was her hand shaking? She gripped the gun as tightly as possible, and she turned that corner, her arm straight up in front of her steadied by her left hand, ready to shoot. And then just as the monster lunged at her, she sat upright in her bed in a pool of sweat, her breath coming out in choked pants.

This was the third time this week that Emma had woken up having a nightmare. She couldn't always remember much of it, but she definitely knew what it was about. PTSD was a real thing, but no matter how many times her friend, Caroline, tried to encourage her to seek counseling for it, she just couldn't. She couldn't relive the story over and over sitting on some couch in some nondescript office. It was bad enough that it had taken up residence in her head, but uttering the words that were bathed in darkness and fear was just too much for her.

The reality of what had happened just a few months ago was still so shocking to her that she couldn't think about it much during the day. She was able to push the feelings and memories aside during her waking hours, but in her dreams they took center stage. She relived the scenario over and over and over again. She often became trapped in her dream, and she was so thankful when her brain would wake her up in a panic because it meant she could escape the terror.

As she did most nights, she got out of the bed, slipped on her robe and walked out onto the small deck on the back of the cottage. It faced the beach, and the sound of the ocean waves soothed her. Not enough, but a little. Each wave gave her a millisecond break, just enough to catch her breath before the memories would catch up with her yet again.

She loved the smell of the the salty sea air, and the fine mist that would come off the ocean during different parts of the day woke her up enough so that she didn't fall back asleep and start the dream all over again. Most nights, she might have gotten three hours of sleep, and it was starting to wear on her.

But what could she do? Life had happened. There was nothing that was going to take away the memories of that fateful night. And her punishment for making that decision was going to haunt her until the day she died. If it didn't haunt her while she was awake, it **hunted** her in her dreams. She felt as if those memories were chasing her night after night.

For a while, she could confide in Steve. He understood. He tried to console her, tell her that she did the right thing. But she didn't do the right thing in her mind. Even though she was cleared of any wrong doing, she could never go back to her job as a police officer. She saw everything differently, and she hadn't even been on duty that night.

Most of her career, she had known that being an officer didn't really suit her. She was much more of a creative type, loving to paint and write and even dance a little bit in high school. After considering the military to get away from her family stress, she opted instead to go into law enforcement. Something inside of her needed the adrenaline at the time, but these days she'd avoid that feeling at any cost. Now, she just wanted peace, yet it seemed to be the most elusive creature on earth.

She had done well in her career for a long time, but then the worst happened. She never really wanted to talk about it with anyone. Truthfully, she wished that she could stop thinking about it and never have to speak about it, but it seemed to be a part of her now. Like an extra arm hanging off of her body, making her heavier and dragging her down.

She pulled her robe tightly around her and walked down onto the dark beach. It was so remote and deserted, and nighttime made it feel even more so. A blanket of stars hung above her in the sky, and she stared up at them wondering if there was life beyond the planet earth. Maybe if she was on some other planet or in some other dimension, she wouldn't be suffering so much now. If you traveled to a different planet, did your history go with you? Or did you truly get a fresh start? Now she was just delusional from lack of sleep.

There was a rock on the beach where she liked to sit, just to get closer to the water. It was so clear tonight that the moon was dancing off the waves as they slowly rolled into shore. There was just something about the ocean that she loved. It felt like each wave was a renewal, a new beginning. Oh, how she wished she could get a new beginning in her own life.

But she didn't deserve it. She had taken a life. She had always known as a police officer that it was a possibility that might happen, but the way it happened wasn't something that she expected. How would she ever get over what she had done?

So she'd run away from her old life in an effort to start a new one, even if it was running a lighthouse on a tiny island out in the middle of nowhere. But so far, she hadn't outrun anything. No, her fears and regrets had come along for the ride like an uninvited guest.

Her grandmother used to say that houseguests and fish started to smell after three days. But she wanted to add something new to that list- regrets. They started to smell too.

Sometimes, just for a brief moment, she thought about walking out into the ocean until she couldn't walk anymore. Not that she wanted to hurt herself. Not really. But she wondered if the universe wanted that. She wondered if the fact that she had taken a life meant that she should give up her own. A person has a lot of dark thoughts when they live in dark places.

CHAPTER 4

*J*ulie finished making the coffee and then straightened the bistro chairs in the café area. It was an early morning at the bookstore because tourist season was now in full swing, and she had to make sure they were ready. Dixie would be coming in soon, and they would go over that week's planning and the upcoming spring festival that would be the highlight of the season in Seagrove.

The spring festival always brought out a lot of tourists and locals alike. Seagrove loved to have festivals at least four times a year. And then there was the local farmers' market that was open every Saturday. Julie loved to go to that, and Lucy often went along with her to pick out things for the inn. The community atmosphere was what she loved most about her adopted hometown.

She was tired this morning, having been up late talking to her daughter about her upcoming wedding and trying to figure out the guest list. Meg was going back-and-forth between wanting to have a big wedding and a small, intimate one. Her ping-ponging was starting to stress Julie out. She liked to have a plan, and she liked to have one early. Meg was much more of a fly by the seat of her pants kind of personality, much like her father.

"Good morning!" Dixie said, grinning from ear to ear as she burst through the front door, almost flinging the little metal bell across the room.

"Goodness gracious! You just about gave me a heart attack! Did you take extra medication this morning or something?" Julie held her hand to her heart, feeling it banging against her sternum like a jackhammer.

"Sorry, honey! I am just so excited this morning I can hardly contain myself!"

"What on earth happened?"

Dixie smiled, dropped her purse on the table and then put both of her hands on Julie's upper arms. "Get ready for this! I can't believe what I found out when I checked my email this morning!"

"That they have reserved your spot at the funny farm?" Julie teased.

"No, they wouldn't be able to handle me there. Anyway, I reached out to Charlotte McLemore's agent a few days ago."

"The author? Why?"

"Well, I told her just how much I love her books, and how everybody around here is just crazy over them. Well, everybody except for you who hasn't read one yet."

"I've been a little busy."

Dixie nodded. "I know, sugar. But you really have to read these books. I have never gotten so attached to characters in my entire life! Anyway, I asked her agent if she might be willing to come here and do a book signing and maybe an appearance at the spring festival!"

"The spring festival? That's next weekend."

Dixie smiled and clapped her hands together. "I know, and she said yes! She doesn't go on her big tour for another few weeks, so they said this would be a great little stop before they get started on the official tour."

"So she's coming here? Next week?"

"Yes, she is! And we can start marketing it all over town. This place is going to be overwhelmed with tourists and locals and probably people who drive in from other cities and states. It's Charlotte McLemore, for goodness sake's!"

Julie stood there looking at her, unable to understand why she was so excited over this particular author. I mean, they had a store full of books. She had never seen Dixie so amped up over meeting anyone, except for that time that she explained how she ran into Burt Reynolds down on the beach twenty years ago. Julie still didn't believe that story.

"Okay… That's great. I'm so glad that you're excited and that it's going to bring possible business here to the bookstore…"

"Julie, you simply have to read one of her books before she comes. You must be well-versed so she knows how thrilled we are to have her here."

"I don't have time to read a book. Do you know how busy I am? I got four hours of sleep last night."

"Honey, I have offered over and over to help you. You keep telling me no. But right now, I'll take whatever you need off your hands so you have time to read one of these books. You won't be the same after you do."

Julie really did want to know what all the fuss was about. She liked to read, but she definitely wasn't one of those people who could devour ten books in a week. Or a month. Or really even a year.

"Fine. Which one should I read?"

Dixie walked over to the table and picked one up, handing it to Julie. If there was one good thing about owning a bookstore, it was that she could take a book home for free. As long as she brought it back looking new, they could still sell it.

"Now, what can I help you with?"

"You know what? My daughter is about to get on my last nerve, so maybe you could get her to make a decision about whether she wants a big wedding or small one because she can't seem to figure that out."

Dixie chuckled. "I will talk to Meg. I'll get that all worked out for you in a jiffy!"

As Julie walked over to the bistro table and sat down with her new book, she wondered if she'd be able to keep her eyes open long enough to read it. But if it was as good as everybody said it was, she was looking forward to a little escape.

William was starving. Today had been a long one with two fishing charters and a group of fraternity brothers who wanted to be taken out on the boat for photos. He'd had a granola bar for breakfast, no lunch and now it was almost dinner time.

Janine had offered to bring him something, but he knew she was busy with a new yoga class she'd added to her schedule. He didn't want to disrupt her day, so he'd gone without. She was keeping Vivi this afternoon, so he was on his own for an early dinner.

As he walked down the sidewalk toward the cafe, he noticed Janine standing in the grass in the square, Vivi running around at her feet. Janine was smiling and laughing. He could hear her infectious giggles from across the square. Opting to watch her for a few minutes, he ducked behind a tree.

She was the most beautiful woman he'd ever seen in real life, and sometimes he couldn't believe she was his. From her beautiful curly hair to her fiery independent streak, he loved everything about her. Sure, they had their moments of arguing over silly things like any couple, but there was never a time where he thought of being without her.

He observed her with Vivi as they both fell to the ground in a pile of high-pitched giggles. Janine didn't care if others looked at her. She was content with being joyful and having a good time, even if it meant laying on her back, kicking her legs in the air to copy what Vivi was doing.

Suddenly, William felt an overwhelming urge to grab her by the hand and walk her to the justice of the peace. She'd be the best wife and mother. They'd talked about possibly adopting at some point, and William was filled with excitement about having that future with her.

What was he waiting for? Was his mother right? Should he make the jump and propose to her?

She deserved a grandiose proposal, but he wasn't exactly the most creative guy in the world when it came to planning romantic dates. What if he disappointed her?

"William?"

Lost in thought, he hadn't noticed Julie walk up behind him. "Oh. Hey there," he said, stammering.

"Are you hiding behind a tree?" she asked, smiling.

"Maybe."

"Why are you hiding from Janine?"

He looked back at the two of them who were now chasing each other and playing some form of tag. "I wasn't exactly hiding. I just saw her and Vivi playing and wanted to watch them for a few minutes."

Julie smiled. "Why do I find this whole scene so incredibly cute?"

He turned around and looked at her, his back against the tree trunk. "I don't know because I'm definitely not cute. I am a strong, confident man," he said, sticking out his chest and smiling.

"Well, confident man, why are you hiding behind this tree where your girlfriend can't see you?"

He looked down at his feet. "It seems that my mother overheard your conversation with Dawson the other day."

Julie furrowed her eyebrows, obviously trying to recollect one of many conversations she had probably had with her husband in recent days. "What did she overhear exactly?"

"That Janine wants to get married."

William watched her face for some kind of reaction, but she held it in well. She pursed her lips tightly and then laughed under her breath. "I'm going to have to have a word with Miss Dixie when I see her next."

"Don't be mad at her. She wasn't trying to over-hear on purpose, but when she did, she ran with it."

"Look, this is your and Janine's business. Nobody else's. And I shouldn't have even been talking about it with Dawson."

"He's your husband. You can talk to him about anything."

"Everybody's relationship has its own course, William. You shouldn't feel pressured just because of what your mother said."

He looked at her for a long moment. "Is what she said true? Does Janine really want to get married?"

Julie shook her head. "Oh no. I'm not getting in the middle of this. I shouldn't have been talking so openly about it so Dixie could overhear me."

She started to walk away but William lightly pulled on her arm. "Please. Just tell me. I don't want to propose and look like a complete idiot when she says no."

"Do you honestly think she would say no?"

"Listen, I've had a lot of bad experiences with women in my life. I don't take anything for granted."

She looked up into his eyes, putting her hands over his. "Janine isn't other women. She loves you with everything she has, and I've never seen her so happy and content. She's not going anywhere, William. So whatever you've experienced in the past with other women who may have let you down, that isn't my sister."

"I know. You're right. I guess the only way to find out if she'll marry me is to ask her. Now I just have to figure out how and then find the courage."

Julie smiled and then kissed him on the cheek. "I know whatever you do will be perfect. You know Janine very well. Just do it with your full heart. You can never go wrong with that."

She walked around the other side of the tree and then ran toward her granddaughter. Vivi giggled loudly as she broke free from Janine and ran to Julie. He continued looking at them from behind the tree until Janine turned around with her back facing him. He took that moment to quickly get back to the sidewalk and continue his walk to get dinner. He needed some time to think, and low blood sugar was starting to set in.

Janine walked down the gravel road leading to the cottage. Sometimes she just liked walking home from work even though it was a pretty long way from town. Today she just felt like clearing her mind, especially after spending so much time playing with Vivi in the square.

When she played with her great-niece, sometimes it left her with a hole in her heart when they parted ways. She longed for a life like her sister had. Husband, kids, and even one day grandkids.

Moving quickly through her forties, she realized that she had started giving up on some of those dreams years ago. When it was obvious that the right man just wasn't in her path yet, she figured that she may never have kids. Now, especially after watching Julie and Dawson adopt Dylan, she knew that a child didn't have to be biologically hers. She adored that little boy just as much as she did Colleen and Meg.

Most women felt their biological clock ticking in their thirties, and Janine had felt that somewhat back then. But she had been far too busy traveling the world with her yoga to give it much thought. In reality, maybe she was running from those feelings all along.

Now, she was with William and she adored him. She truly couldn't see a future that William wasn't a part of. But she wondered if he felt the same long-term feelings for her. He had said so many times, but here they were, still living separately, still not married. There must've been a reason he wasn't making the effort of proposing.

She tried not to feel bitter or resentful. After all, they hadn't been dating a super long time. It wasn't his responsibility to propose if he didn't feel it was the right thing to do. Maybe she would end up being one of those single women who adopted, not that there was anything wrong with doing that. It just wasn't her vision. She saw herself with a husband who loved her and a house with a white picket fence. It was so traditional and so unlike Janine.

Just before the turn to the cottage, she looked up ahead and saw the lighthouse. For once, it was lit up and it stood out in a beautiful way against the sky. It was getting close to sunset, and she wondered how Emma was doing since tomorrow was opening day for tours.

Deciding that she wasn't quite ready to be alone for the evening, she continued walking straight until she came to the lighthouse. She saw Emma coming down the stairs and walking out of the lighthouse. She imagined that she was probably frantic trying to get everything ready for the big opening.

"How's it going?" Janine called to her. Emma, obviously startled, stopped in her tracks, her hand over her heart. "Oh, gosh, I'm so sorry if I scared you."

She paused for a moment before she finally seemed to relax. "It's okay. I'm just still kind of getting used to my surroundings."

Janine thought about that one memory that she wanted to forget more than anything when she got attacked several years ago. It made her wonder if Emma was feeling something similar, being a woman basically alone on an island.

"I know it must be difficult being out here by yourself. My niece lives with me, so at least I'm not alone. The island is completely safe, of course, but it can still make you worry a little bit when you're a woman alone and new in town."

Emma walked closer. "I'm pretty confident in my ability to take care of myself," she said. There was something behind her words, but Janine couldn't put her finger on what it was. She seemed both scared and tough at the same time.

"So, the big opening is tomorrow?"

Emma nodded. "Yes, it is. I'm not nearly as nervous as I thought I would be, although I am a bit concerned that I might forget some of the script that Roger gave me to say on tours. I've never met someone who knew so much about the history of an area."

Janine smiled. "I've met him before. His wife comes to some of my yoga classes from time to time. And you're right, he's very serious about his historical facts. I recall one time getting cornered by him after class while he explained to me little known facts about the Civil War and what happened in this area. Interesting, but a wee bit exhausting when you've been teaching yoga for several hours."

Emma laughed. That was the first time she'd seen her really loosen up since they met her. "I can totally see him doing that. But, he seems like a nice guy. I haven't quite pegged Henrietta yet."

Janine chuckled under her breath. "Henrietta is an acquired taste. She has become best friends with my mom who, as you know, is also an acquired taste."

"She's definitely something else."

"Oh, honey, it's okay if you call it like it is. My mother is a bit of a difficult person, but she tries. Or, I should say *sometimes* she tries."

"Would you like to come in for a cup of coffee?"

Janine was surprised that she was inviting her in given how much she probably had on her plate for the big opening. She also didn't want to be rude, but if she was being honest with herself, a little adult company would be welcome. Spending time with Vivi was fun, but she didn't really have any friends on the island to hang out with that weren't directly related to her.

"Sure. I mean I don't want to impose since I know you're busy."

Emma shook her head. "Pretty much everything that I need to get done for tomorrow has already been done. I mean, there's not a whole lot you have to do when it comes to a lighthouse. All of the heavy lifting of remodeling it has been done, and I've memorized my script. Now it's just a waiting game, and honestly I could use the company to distract myself."

"Great. I'd love to have coffee," Janine said as Emma turned and started walking toward the cottage. Janine followed her, excited that she was getting to make a new friend. Maybe she and Emma wouldn't hit it off, but if they did then she would be happy to have someone to hang out with from time to time.

Of course, she loved being with William, but women needed friends. They needed to vent about their lives to another person who could understand. After all, a woman's journey was very different from a man's.

CHAPTER 5

*A*s they walked into the house, Emma immediately second-guessed herself. What on earth was she thinking inviting Janine in? What if she started asking questions that Emma didn't want to answer? What if she said something that revealed her past?

"Excuse the mess. I'm still trying to get this place set up. I need to do a little shopping for home decor," Emma said.

"Oh please, your place is cleaner than mine. It seems like I'm never home these days. I'm either with my boyfriend or my sister or at work. Tonight I even did some babysitting for my niece."

"Sounds wonderful to have all of those people around you," Emma said as she poured water in the coffee pot. She pointed for Janine to have a seat at the kitchen table.

"It's great. I spent so many years traveling around by myself, teaching yoga in just about every corner of the world. It's nice to have roots again."

"So you did a lot of traveling? That sounds really fun. I've pretty much stayed on this side of the United States for my whole life. I'd like to see some other places eventually."

"Do you have someone special in your life?"

Emma shook her head. "I used to. But it didn't work out."

She prayed that Janine didn't ask any additional questions about her personal life since she really hadn't prepared any answers. But Janine struck her as someone who had been through her share of dark moments, and she felt an immediate kinship with her for some reason.

"I'm really blessed to have my boyfriend, William. I went through a lot of relationships that were definitely not good for me."

"I understand how that is. My last boyfriend was a wonderful man, but there was just too much water under the bridge. A lot of memories that I would rather forget, if you know what I mean."

Why was she opening up? Why was she starting to say things that were only going to lead people to ask more questions about her past?

"Well, enough talk about that sort of thing," Janine said, smiling. "Do you have any family that will be coming to see the lighthouse?"

"No, not really. The only family I ever really had was my grandmother and my mother, and they've both passed away. So, it's just me."

Janine looked at her, a compassionate expression on her face. "Well, what you'll learn about Seagrove is that we all become family. No matter what your background, you are going to be enveloped by the wonderful people of this area."

Emma smiled. "I hope so. This is the first time I've ever just moved away to someplace where I don't know anyone. But eventually I think I'd really like that sense of community."

Janine reached across the counter and patted her on the hand. "I know it's hard to start over some-where new. I felt that way even though I had family here when I arrived. We were all pretty estranged at that point. But you're going to do great here."

"It's hard to imagine that you had any kind of fracture in your relationship with your sister."

Janine chuckled under her breath. "Oh, that was a work in progress for a very long time. But now we're good. She's my best friend."

"I have a best friend back home. Her name is Caroline. She keeps begging me to come back."

"Do you regret moving here?"

"No. I feel peaceful here for the first time in a long time. I mean I still have my moments…" She had almost said too much. What was she thinking? If she started mentioning nightmares, Janine was surely going to ask more questions.

"Look, I understand when we have things in our past that are dark and upsetting, it's really hard to start a new life. I was attacked a few years ago when I was teaching yoga on an island. I didn't tell anyone what happened, and I tried to keep it hidden. But, over time, all it did was separate me further and further from my loved ones. And they thought I was doing things for one reason when it was really because I had this severe trauma I was keeping a secret."

Emma swallowed hard, doing everything within her power not to well up with tears. It was the first time anyone really gave words to her thoughts. "I'm so sorry that happened to you," was all that she could choke out. Janine met her eyes for a long moment, and it was obvious that she was already aware of the fact that Emma was hiding her own trauma.

"Thank you. I went through a lot of therapy, and I still have to go at times, but I'm a lot better now. I found that pushing it down all of those years just made me miserable. Sometimes, those things that we try to keep in the dark start to eat away at our souls. As soon as we bring them out into the light, they dissipate. They lose their power. And that allowed me to get my power back."

Emma smiled. "I'm happy for you. Now, why

don't we have that cup of coffee? I thought this machine would never finish brewing!"

As she hurried to pour the cups of coffee and stop the conversation, Emma couldn't help but feel great relief that she had met Janine. Even though she never planned to tell her what was causing her so much pain, it was nice to know that she had someone who truly understood what she was going through.

Julie, Meg and Colleen walked up the pathway toward the lighthouse. They could've driven Julie's car, but today there were already so many cars on the island going to the lighthouse opening. In fact, Julie couldn't believe how many vehicles were passing them on the gravel road. Normally, it was very rare to see another car moving on this road, but she realized she'd better get used to some level of traffic now that the lighthouse was open.

They had intended to go on the first tour of the day, but Julie was so exhausted between work and wedding planning for Meg that she just didn't have it in her. Plus, Vivi had spent the night with her and had kept the whole household up. Apparently Dawson had slipped her way too much sugar after dinner time.

"I can't believe how many people are here!" Colleen said, looking ahead of them at the parking lot adjoining the lighthouse property.

"It's kind of sad. I don't really want this many people on the island all the time," Julie said.

"Maybe it will be good business for the inn," Meg said, always choosing to look at the bright side.

"So Christian is taking Vivi on a little daddy daughter date?" Julie asked.

"Yes. I think they are going to the park and then to get ice cream. And I have to admit that I'm glad to get a little time off today."

"How's work going?" Colleen asked.

"It's fine. I enjoy working at the college, but I'm not sure it's where I want to be long-term. We'll see."

"Have you thought any more about the wedding invitations?" Julie asked.

Meg stopped in her tracks and looked at her mother. "Mom, I thought we agreed that we're not going to talk about the wedding today. We're just taking a nice, peaceful tour of the lighthouse and then getting lunch. You promised."

"Sorry. It's just that it's your wedding, and it's coming up quickly. There's so many decisions you still haven't made, honey."

"We will get it done. Keep your promise," she said before she started walking again.

Even though she was the smaller in stature of her two daughters, Meg had the stronger personality.

She was also way more stubborn than Colleen had ever been.

"Okay. But I can't promise I won't talk about it at lunch."

Meg rolled her eyes. "Oh, Mom…"

"Let's change the subject," Colleen said. "So, Tucker is busy working on Christmas toy ideas. This is going to be an amazing fourth quarter."

"But it's only spring time," Meg said.

"You would be surprised at how far in advance toy companies have to plan for a Christmas selling season."

They finally arrived at the parking lot. Julie looked up at the beautiful blue sky. The black and white striped lighthouse set against it perfectly and looked like a postcard.

"Have you met Emma yet?" Julie asked.

"No. I haven't had a chance because of working so much. But Aunt Janine said that she's really sweet," Colleen said.

"Yeah, she seems to be really nice. Of course, your grandmother wants to know her entire life history. She's convinced that she's harboring some deep, dark secret," Julie said, laughing.

"Well, I wouldn't expect anything less of Grandma, She should've been a private investigator," Meg said.

They stood in line to get their tickets and then

finally arrived at the door to the lighthouse. At first, Julie didn't see Emma anywhere. She assumed that she was finishing up with a group before them and would be down shortly. Sure enough, several people exited the building and then Emma was standing at her podium.

"Oh, hey, Julie! I'm so glad you got to come today," Emma said, smiling.

"We planned to come this morning but we just couldn't make it work. These are my daughters, Colleen and Meg," Julie said, pointing at each of them.

"So nice to meet you both."

"I know we haven't met, but you look so familiar to me," Colleen said. She squinted her eyes and tilted her head like she was really trying to figure it out. Emma looked slightly uncomfortable.

"I'm not sure why that would be. I'm new around here, and I haven't even had a chance to go into town yet."

"I guess some people just look familiar."

"Let me take your tickets, and we will get started," Emma said, barely making eye contact. Julie chalked it up to just being nervous with the line of people behind them.

The next twenty minutes consisted of walking up the spiral staircase and feeling her legs burn more than they ever had in her life. As she listened to

Emma recite all the facts about the area and the lighthouse restoration, Julie found herself worrying that she needed to get more physical exercise. Her legs felt like they were literally going to burn right off her body. Lots of squats were in her future.

When they got to the top, Emma gave them all some time to take pictures of the view and really take it all in. Then, they were right back down the stairs so that she could take up the next group.

"Thanks so much for the tour," Julie said. "You must have superhuman leg muscles to be able to do this all day."

Emma leaned closer. "Trust me, I'm going to be soaking in an Epsom salt bath tonight and taking as many pain relievers as I can get away with."

Julie laughed. "Listen, why don't you come over for dinner this evening? You're going to be exhausted from all of this, and I would love to serve you a home-cooked meal."

She considered it for a moment. "You know what? I think I might just take you up on that."

"Oh, good! I think Lucy is making pot roast tonight. Is that okay with you?"

Emma nodded. "That would be wonderful."

"Excellent. Let's say seven o'clock?"

"That should work perfect. This place closes at six, so that will give me time to take a shower and head over to the inn."

Julie smiled and walked back toward Colleen and

Meg who were waiting in the parking lot. As they walked back down the pathway, she was happy to have had this time with her daughters. It wasn't often that they hung out together anymore what with all of them working so much of the time. But she also wondered about Emma. Did she have family? Or was she all alone?

Julie knew what it felt like to move to a new area and not know anyone. She wanted to do anything she could to make sure that Emma had a support system just like the one she had been blessed with when she moved to Seagrove. People became family very quickly, and she was hoping to extend that kindness to her new neighbor.

Colleen sat in front of the café with Janine, sipping on an expensive coffee drink and catching up. It seemed like they never got time to just sit and chat anymore. All of the women in the family were busy running their businesses or taking care of their families. Of course, Colleen didn't have a family yet, but she was looking forward to the day that she and Tucker would get married and settle down. For now, she was happy running their business and dreaming about the future.

"I swear she just looks so familiar," Colleen said.

"Maybe she just has that kind of face. You know, some people just look familiar for no real reason."

Colleen took a bite of her biscotti and then dipped it into her coffee. "I guess it's possible. She seems like a nice person. Definitely not a serial killer or anything."

Janine laughed. "You really watch too much of that true crime stuff now. What got you interested in that?"

Colleen shrugged her shoulders. "I don't know. Tucker and I started watching a documentary one night, and I've just been interested in that kind of stuff ever since. I think I just like to know what makes the human mind tick."

"Well, you can have it. I don't like any of that dark stuff. Especially not at night time when I have to go to bed."

"What's this about going to bed?" William said as he walked up to the table. Colleen loved to see the two of them together. He adored her aunt, and she wanted nothing more than for Janine to finally be happy and settle down. She had been absent from the family for so many years when she was traveling and estranged from Colleen's mother. Now, it just seemed like the time was right for her to finally put down roots and get married.

"I was just telling Colleen that I couldn't watch that crime stuff that she does. It would give me nightmares."

He leaned down and gave her a quick peck on the lips. "I don't know, some of that stuff is interesting. I prefer to listen to the podcasts because I'm always on the boat."

"Want to sit down? We can get another chair," Colleen offered.

"No, thanks. I actually need to get home and take a shower. I somehow managed to get fish guts all over me today on one of my charters," he said, pulling at his shirt. Colleen scrunched her nose.

"You know, I could've gone the rest of my life without hearing you say that."

"Sorry. I thought you could take it," he said, poking her in the arm. "Besides, I just came by to say hello to my beautiful girlfriend and ask her if she would like to go on a fancy date with me tomorrow night?"

"A fancy date? What's the occasion?" Janine asked, looking up at him.

"Do I have to have a special reason to take you out?"

"I guess not. It's just that we've both been so busy lately that I wasn't expecting something like this."

He walked around behind her and put his hands on her shoulders, squeezing them before pressing his lips to the top of her curly hair. "You just get all dolled up and I will pick you up at six o'clock."

As he started to walk away, Janine called him. "Where are we going?"

He didn't turn around but yelled back, "Just make sure you wear shoes you can dance in."

Janine stared at Colleen, a smile forming on her face. "What is he up to?"

"I don't know, but it sure sounds fun whatever it is."

CHAPTER 6

*E*mma nervously walked down the road toward the inn. Why on earth would she agree to this? It had already been a long, tiring day and now she had to stay on her game while eating dinner with a bunch of strangers.

It was already obvious that some of the women she met were picking up on the fact that she had run away from her old life. Nobody was asking any direct questions, although she was sure that would be coming soon. Julie and Janine's mother wanted to know her backstory, that much was obvious.

As she walked up the front steps, she tried to gather herself. *Just act normal. Just act normal.* She'd been undercover enough times in her career to get through a simple dinner.

Before she could knock, Julie opened the door, a

big smile on her face. "Emma, I'm so glad that you could make it. Come on in!"

As she walked inside, she was struck at how quaint and beautiful the place was. Obviously a historic home, it had been renovated in a way that preserved the history while also still feeling comfortable and modern.

"Thanks for inviting me. It's been a long time since I've had a home-cooked meal. Even back home, it was always takeout."

"Well, we can't have that! In fact, we have a Sunday family dinner just about every week. You are welcome to come anytime."

Emma smiled. "Thank you. I just might take you up on that."

A tall, very good looking man walked around the corner. Emma could tell he had a very easy-going nature about him. She assumed that he was Julie's husband.

"Emma, I'd like you to meet Dawson, my husband."

She reached her hand out and shook his. It was large and rough, and she could definitely tell that he probably worked with his hands quite a bit. "Nice to meet you. Thank you for having me over for dinner tonight."

He waved his hand. "One thing you'll learn about our little island is that everybody is family. You're always welcome in our home."

"Dawson grew up here. This home actually belonged to his grandmother, and he renovated it himself before opening it as an inn."

"Well, that's impressive. It's a beautiful place, and you have such a wonderful stretch of beach."

"Yes, we do. We spend quite a lot of time out there."

"I don't blame you. I would spend all of my time out there if I were you."

Dawson chuckled. "You don't have such a bad place there yourself. I'm sure the view from the lighthouse is absolutely stunning. I can't wait to come for a tour. I've just been so busy lately that I don't know when I can schedule it, but I promise I'll come by and pay for a ticket."

"It's a stunning view, for sure. I am very blessed to live there."

"Dinner's ready," a woman said, poking her head out from another room.

"Thanks, Lucy. We'll make our way into the dining room," Julie said.

"We better hurry up. You know how ornery she gets if we let the food get cold," Dawson said with a laugh.

As they walked into the dining room, a little boy came running from seemingly nowhere and plopped down at the table.

"Dylan, that was very rude. You don't run

through the dining room, especially when we have a guest here."

The little boy hung his head. "Sorry."

"Thank you. Now, why don't you say hello to Miss Emma. She's running the lighthouse tours now."

He looked up at her, his eyes wide. "You get to go inside the lighthouse?"

Emma smiled. "All day, every day. Have you seen it yet?"

"No. I have to go to stupid school all day. But mom said that we can go soon."

Julie looked at him. "Don't say stupid. That's not nice. And when he finishes his science project, his reward will be going up in the lighthouse. I told him that my new friend, Emma, might tell him a super secret fact about the lighthouse that nobody else knows."

Emma chuckled. "Well, I guess Emma should start finding out some new facts before then, huh?"

She was surprised at how easy it was to blend in with a family she had only just met. As Lucy brought the food in and everybody made their plates, the conversation was easy. She felt like she had known them forever, and that was a testament to just how kind and welcoming they were. How she wished that she had her own family like that with a handsome, sweet husband, and a perky little boy to keep her on her toes. It was what she had always wanted, a stable and happy family. Unfortunately, she had never really experienced that. Although she'd adored her mother, they didn't get to have a picture perfect postcard life. It had been a financial struggle, and her mom had worked a lot when she was a kid.

"So, how are you liking Seagrove so far?" Julie asked.

"Honestly, I haven't been anywhere past the lighthouse yet. I've been so busy trying to get everything ready that I haven't even gone into town."

Julie put her fork down, her eyes wide. "You haven't gone to town? Well, that's it. You must come to the bookstore. And my mom's bakery. We can make sure that you go when she's not working," she said with a laugh.

"I would love to come to town. I promised Janine that I'd come take one of her yoga classes."

"That would be great for you. I'm sure you need to unwind from all the stress of starting a new job in a whole new place. I totally understand what that feels like."

"You do? So you're not from here originally?"

"Oh, no. My story in a nutshell is that my husband of twenty-one years decided that he needed a younger model. We were supposed to be buying a beach house somewhere else and he came home from a business trip and dropped a bombshell that he was in love with someone else and had a son."

"Are you serious? He had a kid you didn't even know about?"

"Yes, it was quite a shock. I needed a new fresh start and I was alone, so I picked the cottage where Janine now lives, site unseen, and moved here. It was quite a whirlwind, and I'm not sure it's something I would ever have the bravery to do again, but it turned out to be the best decision I ever made." She looked at Dawson, reached over and squeezed his hand. Then she looked in the other direction and squeezed Dylan's hand.

"So how many years ago was that?"

"Oh just a couple. Turned out that the cottage was in shambles. I had to hire a local contractor, and that was Dawson. We struck up a friendship and then it became more. And then we found out about Dylan who was in foster care at the time. He just became our son very recently."

"Wow! I had no idea. You guys look like you've been a family forever. I just assumed that Dylan…" She didn't want to finish her sentence by saying that she assumed he was theirs. Obviously, he was theirs. Just not biologically.

"I like to think that we were a family meant to be together by God," Dawson said, smiling.

"I'm sure you're right." Emma took a sip of her sweet tea. "Congratulations on making such a wonderful life for yourself, Julie."

"It is a wonderful life. And once I came here, I

started working at the bookstore and then became part owner. And then we opened the inn. So, I'm just saying that so many things happened out of such a lonely beginning. When I first moved here, I thought for sure I'd made a mistake. I almost turned around and went back to my country club lifestyle."

"What's a country club?" Dylan asked. They all laughed.

"It's something that I would never do again," Julie said, ruffling the hair on top of his head.

They continued talking, and Emma was so thankful that nobody was asking her personal questions. It was like they knew that she wouldn't be comfortable answering them anyway. She enjoyed the relaxing way they were able to talk without worrying about somebody springing something on her. It was the first time she felt this peaceful in well over a year, and probably more.

"Dessert?" Lucy asked, poking her head out of the kitchen once again. She hadn't eaten with the family, saying that she had snacked too much while she was cooking dinner.

"No, thank you. I'm stuffed," Emma said. Julie said the same, but Dawson and Dylan were more than happy to accept the chocolate muffins that she had made.

"Do you want to go sit out by the water and maybe have a glass of wine while these guys continue shoveling sugar into their faces? Julie asked, winking at her husband.

"Sure. It's a beautiful night, so I would enjoy a nice glass of wine."

A few minutes later, the two women were sitting in two white Adirondack chairs on the beach. The constant sound of the waves coming in and out and the warm ocean breeze made Emma feel like she just wanted to close her eyes and stay there forever. Even though she was on the ocean when she stepped out the back of her own cottage, there was just something about the little beach that Julie and Dawson had that felt so comfortable and right. She stared out over the water as she took a sip of her wine, noticing the moonlight dancing on each of the waves and then shattering into a million pieces as it hit the shore.

"Thank you for dinner. It was wonderful."

"You're welcome. Lucy does all the heavy lifting. I like to cook, but she rarely lets me in the kitchen," she said, giggling.

"It sounds like you're a very busy woman anyway. I'm sure you enjoy the extra help."

"I do. I complain, but I secretly love it."

"You have a great family, Julie. You're very blessed."

She took a sip of her wine and nodded. "I am very blessed, for sure. Can I ask you something?"

Emma froze in her seat, her breath catching in

her throat. Was she going to start asking her personal questions? She felt the sudden urge to bolt and run straight back to lighthouse.

"Of course."

"Have you ever heard of an author named Charlotte McLemore?"

Emma let her breath out. "I think I've heard of her in passing. From a couple of friends. Why?"

"Everybody is talking about her books, and I have one I'm supposed to start reading but every time I get started, I get distracted by something else. I promised myself that I would sit in bed tonight and at least read the first chapter. If I like it, I'll continue."

"Sounds like a good plan," Emma said, laughing. "Every time I try to read in bed, I fall asleep within minutes."

"Same here. I've given Dawson permission to elbow me until I finish chapter one."

She really enjoyed talking to Julie. Emma really understood her. Even though she hadn't been married or had a cheating husband, she certainly knew what it was like to run away from her old life and try to start a new one. She hoped that she would be as lucky as Julie had been.

"Well, I better get back. I'm so exhausted from today, and I want to get a really good night of sleep before tours start in the morning. I understand we have a third grade class coming for a field trip."

Julie laughed. "You better get a lot of extra sleep for that."

Emma stood up and gave Julie a quick hug. She was so thankful to already be making new friends. There was just something special about Seagrove Island, and she was thankful that God had somehow led her there. She felt like she had support, even from the people she hadn't met yet.

"I'll see you soon. I want to come by the bookstore."

Julie smiled. "You're going to love this little town. Let it support you, Emma. Whatever situation you came from, you can always find a new start in Seagrove. I am a testament to that."

William couldn't remember a time when he had felt more nervous than he did right now. After picking up Janine, who was dressed for a night on the town, they had gone dancing at an adorable jazz club in Charleston. The whole time they were dancing, he was afraid that she could feel his heart pounding out of his chest. Or could she feel that little black box with the diamond ring shoved down in his dress pants pocket.

Thankfully, she didn't seem to notice. She was too busy dancing, throwing around her thick curly hair to the music. He was so happy to be out with her having a good time. Lately, they had seemed so busy with work that they didn't get to do the fun things they used to.

Now, sitting across from her in the dimly lit restaurant, a single candle between them, he looked at her trying to figure out the words to say. He'd never done this before, after all. Proposing to a woman was something he had always planned to do, but the right woman had never come along. Until Janine.

He kept sneaking glances at her when she wasn't looking. The way that the candlelight danced off her features just made her more beautiful. He didn't even know that was possible. She smiled as she saw someone she knew across the restaurant, holding up her hand and waving at them. They often ran into people that took her yoga classes, and everyone loved her. She put her whole heart into everything that she did, and helping people was the most important part of who Janine was.

"I can't wait to get my food. I'm starving," she said, putting her napkin in her lap. The restaurant was fancier than any one they had ever been to. Cloth napkins and a maître d'. William had to check his credit card to make sure he was going to have enough money to pay for it, and that wasn't something he often had to think about. It was just that expensive. But he wasn't going to spare any expense when it came to proposing to the love of his life.

"Me too," he said.

"Are you okay? You've seemed kind of nervous all night. Is everything all right at work?"

William laughed. "What could possibly go wrong on a boat?"

She shrugged her shoulders. "I don't know. I just figured that something must be going on because we never go out on fancy dates like this, and you seem awfully nervous."

"No. Just happy to be here with you," he said, reaching across the table and holding her hand. Maybe he would do it right now. There was no reason to wait for the dessert. He should just go ahead and do it so that he didn't have to feel nauseous all the way through dinner.

"I love you," she said, smiling at him. Yes, now was the exact right time to do it. It was the romantic moment he'd been waiting for.

"Janine, I need to ask you something…"

Before he could finish his sentence or drop to one knee, the waiter two tables over started banging a fork against a wine glass. Everybody in the restaurant turned to look.

"Ladies and gentlemen, join me in congratulating Sarah and Tate who just got engaged!"

The whole restaurant erupted in cheers and clapping, and William felt like he was going to throw up. He'd missed his chance. There was no way he was going to propose to Janine right after someone else had already done it. He wanted her to have the perfect moment, and this wasn't it.

"Oh, that's so sweet. They look like a really cute couple,"

"Yeah. Cute couple," he said, his words coming out one at a time like he was choking on them.

"Well, before we got interrupted, you said you had a question to ask me?"

She sat there smiling expectantly. Did she know what he was going to ask? Was she assuming?

"Right... Well... I was just going to ask you... If you had any idea what time the spring festival starts?"

She sat there for a moment, her face falling slightly. "Oh. No, but I'm sure Julie knows. I can text her later."

"Great."

The awkward silence that hung between them was as thick as molasses. When the food came, they ate quietly, each of them avoiding eye contact and only talking about the food. How the rolls were nice and hot. How the soup was creamier than they'd imagined it would be. What had he done? He should've just popped the question when he had the chance. Now she was mad or sad or something.

William didn't know what to do. If he proposed now, she was going to think that he was doing it forcibly. That he didn't really want to but felt he had to. And it wouldn't be the romantic gesture that he had planned. No matter how awkward it was, he had to find a different way to propose to her that would be something she would remember forever. A crummy, stupid restaurant wasn't enough for her anyway. He was going to go big the next time.

CHAPTER 7

*J*ulie walked into the bookstore to find Dixie sitting at the table, reading yet another Charlotte McLemore book. Luckily, there didn't seem to be any customers in the store just yet since it was pretty early.

"Good morning," Dixie said, hardly looking up.

"You're reading another one?"

"Yes, I am. And I swear this one is better than the other one. I don't know how she does it. She's like a genius or something," Dixie said, dabbing at her eyes with a tissue.

"You're such a fangirl."

"So, did you read that book?"

Julie scrunched her nose and shook her head. "No. I tried last night but I got one page in, and I fell asleep on Dawson's shoulder. He kept elbowing me, but it didn't do any good. But I'm going to try to read some on my lunch break today."

"Charlotte's coming in just a few days. You've got to get it read or she's going to know it. She's going to realize that you didn't like the book…"

"I never said I didn't like it. I'm just exhausted. By the way, have you talked to Meg about the wedding for me?"

Dixie shrugged her shoulders. "I'm going to do that. I just got so caught up in this book last night that I totally forgot to call her again…"

Julie pulled the book out of her hand. "Young lady, you are not allowed to read anymore of this book until you get your chores done."

Dixie cackled with laughter. "You know I've got a stack of those books right behind me, don't you? I'll just grab another one."

"You wouldn't dare!" Julie said, laughing as she handed the book back to Dixie. "But try to at least get some work done today."

"Well, I've got some bad news on that front. I've actually got a physical therapy appointment in a few minutes. I'll be gone for at least a couple of hours."

"That's okay. I can handle this place by myself." Dixie stood up, walked behind the counter and retrieved her handbag.

"I'll bring you back some lunch from the café. Chicken salad croissant?"

"Yes, and tell Dorothy to go extra heavy on the

chicken. The last time it was more bread than anything else. That new girl doesn't know what she's doing."

Dixie smiled and nodded before walking out the front door. Julie loved the familiarity of living in Seagrove. Everybody knew everybody else. Of course, that also meant that everybody was in everybody else's business, but it still felt like home. Much more like home than any other place she'd ever lived, including where she raised her daughters.

Seagrove was like this strange little hamlet that most people didn't know about, but it was heaven on earth to her. It was where she had found Dawson and Dylan, and it was where she planned to spend the rest of her days.

This time of the morning was her favorite at the bookstore. Even though there were a lot more tourists in town right now, very few of them came to the bookstore until after lunch. It gave her time to tidy up, get the coffee ready for the day and just spend some quiet time with herself. That was something that she didn't get a lot of these days with a young son to raise.

She adored Dylan, of course, but he was high energy and she was getting older. She didn't expect to be raising a little boy at this stage of her life, but she was grateful to be his mom. Still, she enjoyed those moments where she could just sit quietly, close her eyes and take a few deep breaths.

Janine had been trying to coax her back to a yoga class so that she could learn how to calm down a bit, but Julie had been resistant. She knew her sister was the best yoga teacher around, but there was just something about being in a class full of people. She preferred to sit alone when she wanted to rest her mind.

As she finished wiping down the café tables, she heard someone walk through the front door. It was a woman she'd never seen before. She was well dressed for the area. Tall, thin, with beautiful short, red hair and porcelain white skin. She was obviously very high class, as her mother would call it.

"Welcome to Down Yonder Books. Can I help you with anything?"

The woman smiled. "No, thank you. I just wanted to take a look around before I go to a meeting."

"Feel free. You have the run of the place. Not many people come here this time of the morning."

She nodded slightly and then started walking around the store, slowly running her hands across the books on the shelves. Occasionally, she would pick one up, thumb through it and then set it back on the shelf. Julie noticed that she was mostly looking at fiction books.

"What genre do you read?"

"What?" the woman asked, turning around as if she was slightly startled.

"Oh. I was just asking what genre you read. Maybe I could suggest something?"

"Mostly women's fiction. I like really emotional stories about strong women."

Julie smiled. "Well, a lot of people recommend this author named Charlotte McLemore. We have a table full of her books over there."

The woman turned and looked at the table, reaching down to pick up one of the books. "Do you have a particular one that you recommend?"

Julie smiled shyly. "I have to say that I haven't really read any of them. Well, I started one last night because my partner here at the bookstore has been bugging me about it. The author is supposed to be coming here soon for a book signing."

"Oh? So you haven't read any of the books yet?"

"No. I tried to start one last night, but in all honesty I felt like it was a little slow."

"Slow?"

"Yes, and I'm never telling my friend because she won't leave me alone about it. I'm going to try to read it again on my lunch break today."

"So you didn't like it?"

"I can't really say that because I don't know. I only read the first page."

The woman chuckled. "How can you tell anything about a book from the first page?"

Julie leaned against the front counter and crossed her arms. "I just feel like a book should be able to grab you from the very beginning. And the first page was pretty slow. I fell asleep."

"You're not doing a very good sales job," the woman said, laughing.

"Sorry. Everyone loves those books, so I'm sure it's just me."

"I might give one a try. But I saw a different one over here that looked interesting from another author. I think I'll look through that one a little bit first."

"Would you care for a cup of coffee or a muffin?"

Her eyebrows raised. "I would love a cup! What kind of muffins do you have?"

"Well, I have chocolate, blueberry and apple cinnamon. My mom owns the bakery down the street, and she provides them to us."

"I'll take a blueberry muffin."

She walked over and sat down at one of the tables and started looking through the book she had picked up.

Julie finished pouring the coffee and put the muffin on a small white plate before taking it to the table.

"So, is this your first time in Seagrove?"

The woman looked up at her. "It is. Very cute little town."

"You said you have a business meeting here? That's pretty unusual for Seagrove."

"Yes. Just so happens that my business associate

lives here. I'm actually staying over in Charleston, though."

"Oh, darn. My husband and I own an adorable little inn over on the island. I was going to tell you that you might want to consider staying there. It's right on the ocean."

"Really? I'm not too fond of my hotel. Too much traffic noise. Do you have a room available?"

"Of course! Here, I'll write down the information and you can drive over when you leave here if you'd like. My husband is there and can get your room all set up."

She smiled. "That sounds fantastic. I'm looking forward to staying there for a couple of nights."

"Oh, and I hope you'll be here for our spring festival. It starts the day after tomorrow. It's going to be a lot of fun!"

"I might just check that out. Thanks for the hospitality."

Julie walked back behind the register. "I forgot to ask your name?"

The woman looked up and smiled. "Oh, it's Anna."

"Well it's nice to meet you Anna. My name is Julie."

J anine sat there picking at her salad, staring off into the distance. She just couldn't believe what had happened at the restaurant the night before with William. Something just wasn't right.

"Hey, Janine!" Emma said, standing beside her. Janine hadn't even noticed her walk up. She was just too lost in her own thoughts.

"Oh, hey. I figured you'd be over at the lighthouse giving tours today."

"We're actually only open half a day. Something went wrong with the light, and they've got the repair guy up there. We had a field trip group this morning, and I swear one of them unplugged something," she said, laughing. "Mind if I join you?"

Janine smiled and nodded, pointing at the chair across from her. "Please."

"You look a little sad today. Is everything all right?"

"Honestly, I have no idea."

"What can I get you, honey?" the server asked Emma.

"I'll just take a club sandwich and a glass of water. Thanks." She immediately turned back to Janine with a concerned look on her face. "What's going on? I know we just met, but if you need somebody to talk to, it's not like I can gossip. I don't know anybody else really," Emma said, laughing.

Janine smiled. "Last night my boyfriend took me

on a very fancy date. We went dancing and then we went to the most expensive restaurant I've ever been to."

"That sounds nice. So what's wrong?"

"Well, I had the distinct impression that he might have been proposing last night. Another couple in the restaurant even got engaged. But then suddenly something changed. It was like he had second thoughts or cold feet. He barely spoke to me the rest of the night, and he definitely didn't propose."

"I'm sure it's nothing. It sounds like he loves you very much. Maybe he just decided to go a different route."

Janine picked at her food. "I don't know. I'm just ready to start my life with him. I don't understand what happened, and I'm too afraid to ask. I don't want to assume that he was going to propose if he wasn't."

"Maybe just wait it out. See if he does it another way. Guys are weird."

Janine smiled. "They are very weird. I like you, Emma. You've made me feel a little better."

The waitress put Emma's glass of water on the table. "Then my work here is done," she said, taking a long sip.

E mma enjoyed her lunch with Janine, but she had to get back to the lighthouse. The city council really wanted her to work on some flyers that could be handed out at the Spring Festival. Apparently, she would also have a little table with displays about the lighthouse's history and would be doing a raffle for some free tour tickets.

When she had taken the job, she'd assumed it was nothing more than walking people up and down the stairs, telling them random facts. She hadn't intended on doing marketing since it wasn't her forte.

Thankfully, she had been able to talk the city council into buying her a secondhand golf cart so that she didn't have to walk everywhere since she didn't have a car. She had turned in her rental car the day after she arrived on the island.

Roger had delivered the golf cart this morning, and that had allowed her to finally get into the city to have some lunch. She didn't have time to go by the bookstore or the bakery, but it was on her list of things to do very soon.

She hated to admit to herself that she was starting to hit her stride. She felt more at home in Seagrove than she had in a while. Nobody knew her there. Nobody knew her history or what had happened. Nobody knew about her dead mother or her crazy grandmother. Nobody knew about her boyfriend that she left behind or the night that her life changed.

A fresh start was a blessing, and she was starting to enjoy hers more than she thought she would. Instead of holing herself up on the island, she was starting to get out and make friends. She was starting to feel comfortable.

As she rounded the corner down the gravel drive and passed Janine's cottage, she noticed a car sitting in the parking lot at the lighthouse up ahead. It was weird because it was closed for the rest of the day. She assumed maybe it belonged to the contractor who was working on the light, although she thought he should be long gone by now.

As she pulled into the parking lot, she noticed that it was a rental car. Maybe some tourist had shown up for a lighthouse tour not realizing that they were closed for the rest of the day. Perhaps the note she put on the door next to the ticket counter had blown away in the ocean breeze.

She parked her cart and got out, being careful to remember that she was a woman alone on an island. If she screamed, it wasn't likely anyone was going to hear her.

Still, her training as a police officer always kept her in good stead. She knew she could take care of herself, and she always kept a concealed weapon on her. Just part of her job training, although touching a gun made her have flashbacks that she'd rather not experience.

She walked up to the car and saw no one inside. There was also no one standing anywhere near the lighthouse. Now she was feeling a little bit uncomfortable. Perhaps the best thing to do was to get inside of her cottage and lock the door until she could figure out who was lurking around her property.

She got back in her cart and pulled closer to the cottage. As she stepped out of the golf cart, she saw someone off in the distance standing on the beach behind her house. When she looked closer, she knew exactly who it was.

"Steve?"

Her boyfriend - ex-boyfriend - turned around and looked at her.

"Emma! Thank God I found you!" he said, running toward her. He closed the gap between them very quickly, pulling her into a tight embrace and pressing his face into the crook of her neck.

"Why are you here? How did you even find me?" She felt more irritated than she probably should have. He seemed overwhelmed with worry, although she had explained to Caroline that she was okay and that she should relay that information to Steve.

He pulled back and looked at her, his hands on her arms. "I'm a detective, Emma. I can find anybody. The better question is why did you run away without a word? You scared all of us to death!"

"I've been talking to Caroline. I told her that I'm fine."

She turned to walk back towards the front of the house, Steve following close behind. "She said you didn't sound like yourself on the phone. She was worried that you might hurt yourself, so I had to get here as soon as possible."

"Well, I'm really sorry that you wasted a trip, but I'm fine."

He reached for her arm and turned her around. His eyes were starting to fill with tears, and his face was red. She knew the red face was from anger, and the tears were from fear. To be a detective, Steve wore his emotions on his sleeve.

"You're my fiancé. We're supposed to be getting married and living a life together, Emma. How could you just run away like that?"

"Steve, we're not getting married. The girl that you were engaged to died that night. I am no longer her, and I can't marry you." She put the key into the lock of her cottage and walked inside, Steve following behind her. He pushed it closed behind him and stood there like he didn't know what to do.

"It wasn't your fault. Nobody thinks that it was."

"Well, I do. I just don't think I'll ever get over it."

"Emma, he was a bad guy."

"So he deserved to die? I could've chosen to shoot

him in the leg or tackle him. But I didn't. I killed a person."

He looked at her for a long moment before speaking. "Every cop dreads the thought of taking a life. You know that. We had training on that."

"Well training and real life are very different, Steve. And you've never taken a life, so you have no idea. You might've been there that night, but you didn't have to pull the trigger." The reality was that she resented him for sending her in first. He thought he was giving her the gift of solving a big case, but she felt like he threw her into the national spotlight in one swift motion.

"I know, honey, and I wish it had been me. I wish that I could take that weight off of you, but I can't. And if you would just see the counselor…"

She held up her hand. "I don't want to see a counselor. There is no counselor who can tell me how to feel. I'm the one going through it! I don't want to talk about this anymore or think about this anymore. I just want to move on with my life."

"I don't understand. Why would you come to this little island where you don't know anybody?"

"That's exactly the reason why I'm here. I wanted a new job and new friends. I just can't go back. I needed to become a new version of myself, and it's working for me. I'm happy here. Well, as happy as I can be right now."

He looked stunned. "How can you say that?

We've been together for three years. We had plans, Emma. We were going to retire from the force together in a few years and travel. We were talking about opening our own security company."

She felt bad for him. He was so torn up inside, and she just wasn't. She felt almost nothing. She had loved him once, but now when she looked at him all she saw was her old life and she just couldn't conjure up romantic feelings anymore. She walked over to her purse and opened the inside zipper, pulling out her engagement ring. She handed it to him.

"I release you, Steve. You need to find somebody who wants those same dreams with you. I don't ever want to go back there. I don't ever want to be a police officer again, and I don't want to start at a security company. I'm happy right here on this little island running this lighthouse."

He stared at the ring for a long moment before finally taking it from her hand. "You can't run forever, Em. How can you be happy living such a small life like this?"

She smiled slightly. "Just because it's a small life doesn't mean it's not a fulfilling one. People here are just different. I can be myself, my real self, the one that I've been hiding my whole life. I can be a part of a community, and I don't have to be scared. I don't have to be on the defensive. I can just relax and do what I love. I can follow whatever dreams I have right here. I already have friends."

"So, that's it? You're just cutting ties with me and Caroline and the whole community you had back home?"

She swallowed hard. "Caroline will always be my best friend, and I will never cut ties with her. But everything else, I have to let go of. It's like I was a different person before the shooting, and now I'm this person. You wouldn't want to be engaged to her anyway, Steve. She's a stranger to you."

He shook his head. "I think you're making a big mistake. You built a career, and you were going to have a wonderful retirement. I just don't understand any of this."

She walked over to the front door and opened it. "That's the beauty of this freedom I have. Nobody has to understand. I get to choose the life I want, and I've made my choice. I'm sorry, Steve. I never wanted to break your heart. But this is how it has to be for me, and I'm at peace with it. I hope you have a really happy life and you find someone who will love you the way you deserve."

He slowly walked past her and back out onto the porch.

"I wish you all the best, Emma. I know you're broken from what happened, and I truly hope one day you'll get some help for that because you deserve to feel at peace about that too. Goodbye."

As she watched him walk down and get into his rental car, she felt lighter. This was something that should've happened months ago, but she didn't know if she was ready to let go of the relationship when everything else in her life was falling apart. She watched the car disappear down the long gravel street, and she knew that she was finally starting her life over again.

CHAPTER 8

*J*ulie loved having someone stay at the inn. Her whole life, she had enjoyed meeting new people and finding out about their lives. For a long time, she had even considered being a newspaper reporter or a television journalist so that she could go out into the world and ask people questions without them thinking that she was just nosy.

When Anna had agreed to come stay at the inn while she was in Seagrove on business, it made Julie happy to have someone else to talk to. She was enjoying her new friendship with Emma, and she always enjoyed her time with Dawson and Dylan. But the constant in and out of guests was one of her favorite things about living there.

"I hope you enjoyed dinner," Julie said as she sat across from the kitchen table with Anna.

"It was wonderful. I can't remember when I've enjoyed chicken and dumplings so much. Lucy is definitely genius in the kitchen."

Julie nodded. "Yes, she definitely is. So, how long did you say you'll be in Seagrove?"

Anna took a sip of her coffee. "Probably until Monday. I've got some other things coming up that I have to attend to, so I don't think I can stay much past that. I hope it's okay for me to stay here that long?"

Julie laughed. "We have plenty of rooms. Our busy season is starting to pick up, but we don't have nearly as many reservations as we probably should. Once the spring festival is over, that's when we expect to get a rush of tourists in town."

"Spring festival? What's that all about?"

"It actually starts this weekend. We have all kinds of vendors who set up tables, like my mom who owns the local bakery. Of course we have live music, food, games for the kids. It's just a really great time for the town to get together and welcome in spring."

"That sounds really fun."

"Oh, it is! I hope that you get some time to join us. I'd love to introduce you to some of my friends. I mean, I know you're only here on business, but we like to welcome our guests."

"I will definitely try to be there. By the way, don't you have a book to read tonight?"

Julie rolled her eyes. "I've been procrastinating

on that. It's not that I don't want to read it, although it wasn't super interesting to me the first time around."

"Didn't you say you only read part of the first page?"

Julie giggled. "I just get very distracted when I'm reading books. Maybe I should try the audiobook?"

"I don't know. For me, there's just something about the process of reading. I don't do so well with audiobooks."

"I guess I should get on it so I don't fall asleep like I did last night. Is there anything else that you need from me before I head upstairs?"

"No, thank you. I think I'm going to sit out on the porch for a while, maybe make a couple of phone calls. Then I'm going to be heading to bed myself. I've got an early morning meeting tomorrow."

"Yeah, same here. In fact, it's this author that's coming tomorrow for a book signing. I better try to read this thing so I know what I'm talking about," she said with a chuckle.

Colleen leaned against her fluffy pillows and stared at her computer screen. Maybe she did have an actual addiction. She just couldn't stop watching true crime documentaries. It seemed like the streaming services had one after another, and each one seemed more interesting and suspenseful than the last.

"You need to go to bed," Tucker said, his voice booming through the speaker on her phone and startling her.

"Geez, tell me when you're going to say something because you scared the crap out of me!"

They often did this at night where Tucker was at his apartment and she was at the cottage with her Aunt Janine, but they stayed in touch on their phones because they couldn't stand to be apart. Hours would pass while they each watched TV or did household chores, sometimes not saying anything for long stretches of time.

Colleen couldn't wait for the day when they got married and could live in the same house all the time. Of course, they could do that now, but she just wanted some time on her own before settling down with a man again. The whole thing with her former fiancé, Peter, had made her long for a little bit of independence before she started her own family.

And the truth was, she had plenty of time. She was only in her twenties, so it wasn't like her biological clock was ticking very loudly yet. Of course, when she saw her sister getting to be a mother, she did feel herself longing for that sometimes. But definitely not enough to rush into getting married and starting a family so soon.

She and Tucker had some big business goals

before then. The Christmas selling season would be coming again in a few months, and it was going to be a challenge but a possible financial windfall for both of them.

They had also talked about traveling together and seeing different parts of the world before they finally settled down. She was thankful that she had time and didn't have to worry about being in a hurry for any reason.

"What are you doing?" Tucker asked. She could hear him washing his dishes in the background.

"There's a new documentary I wanted to see. It's about this serial rapist."

"Wow, that sounds like something that is so soothing right before bedtime."

"You're a wimp," she said, laughing.

"I truly don't know how you watch that stuff right before you go to sleep. It would give me nightmares."

"Sometimes it does. I still can't help myself. It's just so interesting."

"Well, I don't want to keep you from your new documentary, so I'm going to hang up and go take a nice hot shower. I'll see you in the morning?"

"See you then. Sweet dreams," she said before hanging up.

She snuggled back into her pillows again, pulled the cover up around her neck and pressed play. As the documentary started, she learned facts about the case.

Apparently there was this man who was raping women in this small town. They couldn't catch him no matter what they did, but he was finally shot and killed by an officer during a standoff.

As she watched about all the different cases, she was so thankful that she didn't live alone. At least having her Aunt Janine there meant that she wasn't as worried being at home alone at night. A lot of these girls had been attacked in their apartments where they lived alone.

As the story went on, she started to learn more about the standoff. About how he had taken a hostage and was trying to blackmail the police. It went on for hours and hours until finally one of the officers snuck into the building and was able to shoot him before he could hurt his hostage.

And that's when Colleen found herself staring at the screen, holding her breath. The officer that shot him was a woman, but that wasn't the part that was so shocking. She knew who that officer was, and she couldn't believe what her eyes were seeing.

She tossed her computer to the side, pausing the documentary as she did, and ran out into the living room. "Aunt Janine!"

Janine came flying out of her bedroom, her curly hair sticking straight up like she'd stuck her finger in a light socket. She had her robe wrapped around her and was holding her chest. "What's going on? Are you hurt?"

Colleen shook her head. "No! I was just watching this crime documentary…"

Janine rolled her eyes and then bent over like she was trying to catch her breath. "Girl, have you lost your mind? You almost gave me a heart attack!"

"You don't understand. There was a female police officer who shot the rapist."

"Okay…"

"We know her!"

"We know who?"

"The police officer!" Colleen was getting more and more frustrated like Janine was supposed to understand what was popping around inside of her own mind.

"You're not making any sense!"

"The police officer that shot the rapist and killed him… It was Emma."

"What? Emma from the lighthouse?"

"Yes! I saw her on the documentary. I've got it paused on my bed. I knew she looked familiar! I must've seen her on the news at some point."

"It was probably just someone who looks a lot like her. Emma keeps a lighthouse. She's not a police officer."

"And how do you know that? Did she tell you what she did before she came here?"

"Well… no… I got the feeling that she left a life

behind that was stressing her out or she had some traumatic event…"

Colleen put her hands on her hips. "You mean like shooting and killing someone?"

"Let me see," Janine said, pointing to Colleen's bedroom.

She followed Colleen into the room. They both sat down on the edge of the bed as Colleen picked up her laptop and pressed play. Sure enough, Emma's face popped back up on the screen again. Colleen pressed pause.

"See? That's definitely Emma."

Janine sat there silently for a moment. "She must be completely traumatized."

"I don't get it. I mean, police officers have to know that they may end up killing someone in the line of duty. Why would that bother her enough to leave her entire life behind?"

"You know, sometimes you think you know how you'll react to a situation. And then you get put in that situation, and it's a lot harder than you think it would've been. Maybe that's what happened."

"What are we going to do?"

"What do you mean what are we going to do? This is none of our business," Janine said, standing up and walking toward the door.

"Aunt Janine, it's obvious that she needs some extra support or help. Running away from it isn't going to be the best thing for her. Surely you know that after the trauma you suffered."

Janine slowly turned. "Say nothing. Don't tell anyone. You don't publicize someone else's trauma."

"I wouldn't do that."

"Let me think about it. If I feel like I need to talk to her, I will. But for now, let her enjoy this new start. That's the best thing we can do for her in this moment."

Julie had never seen Dixie run around so quickly. The book signing was starting in a couple of hours, and they expected the author to show up at any minute. Julie had tried to finish reading the book the night before, but she had fallen asleep about halfway into chapter three. Still, she found herself getting more and more interested in the plot, so that was a good thing. Hopefully the author didn't ask her any specific questions or she was going to be in a pickle.

"Do you think this place looks clean enough?" Dixie asked, standing there with her hands on her hips as she surveyed the entire bookstore. They had been sweeping and scrubbing and tidying up since they got there at seven AM.

"It's fine. We're not being judged on cleanliness.

We're hosting an author who wants to sign books. We're doing her a favor!"

Dixie laughed. "I don't think that's true. Just the fact that she's going to be here means we're going to have all sorts of people lined up outside. It's going to be great for business."

"Maybe so, but they're here to look at her books and meet her. They're not here to buy more books from other authors, or at least I wouldn't think so. Just don't be disappointed if sales don't skyrocket, okay?"

"Where is that clipboard?" Dixie asked, suddenly running around yet again.

"I put it on the table. People will be able to write their emails so that we can send them regular messages about sales and so forth. I've got it handled. You really need to calm down before you end up in the hospital."

Dixie chuckled under her breath. "I haven't been this excited in years. I feel like I'm about to meet Elvis!"

Julie rolled her eyes and laughed. "I think you might be getting a little dramatic."

"I think I'll run to the back and just make sure that we didn't miss a box of books that we can sell. Keep an eye out because she should be here soon."

"Will do, sir," Julie said, saluting her like she was a military leader.

She finished straightening the books on the table

where Charlotte McLemore would be signing. She made sure that their most comfortable chair was pushed up behind it. Although she wasn't nearly as excited as Dixie, she did like the way the woman wrote.

Julie had always wanted to write a novel, and she had been working on one for almost a year now. But it seemed like life was always getting in the way, and she never could get the thing finished. Even if she did, she didn't know who would publish it. All of it seemed like a very involved process, and she wasn't sure if she could take the rejection if people didn't like it.

Still, she wanted to write a novel about a woman like herself who had had the strength to leave a bad situation and start a new life that was even better than she could've hoped for. That was how she saw herself, at least most of the time.

When she looked back at her life over the last couple of years, it was hard to believe she was the same woman who sat with her snooty country club "friends" for lunch every week. She hadn't spoken to those women in a long time, and she had nothing in common with them now.

It felt like she had been a different person back then, like her real self had been buried for so long that she didn't even know she was still in there. Seagrove brought her back to life, and she was forever grateful for that.

The door dinged and she looked up to see Anna standing there. "Well, good morning! I didn't know you were coming by here."

"I love to read, so I thought I'd take a look while I was heading to my appointment."

"Well, we've got plenty of these," Julie said, holding up one of Charlotte's books and laughing.

"Looks like you do! How much did you end up reading last night?"

"I got about halfway through the third chapter before I fell asleep, although I don't think it's the author's fault. The book was actually pretty good, but I was exhausted. I probably shouldn't have had that glass of wine I snuck upstairs."

"Oh, a good glass of wine is always okay."

"Would you like a cup of coffee? I just made a fresh pot."

"No thanks. I had some before I left the inn."

"I hope that your room was to your liking?"

"It was wonderful! I swear that was the most comfortable bed I've ever slept in."

She heard Dixie come out of the storage room in the back. "Oh, I want to introduce you to my friend and business partner."

Dixie appeared behind her, her mouth dropping open and her eyes widening. She looked like she'd seen a ghost.

"Oh my goodness… You're early…"

"Early? Dixie what are you talking about? This is

my new friend, Anna. She's staying at the inn. She's here on business."

Dixie stared at her, her eyebrows furrowed. "Julie, do you not know who this is?"

"Yes, of course I do. I told you this is Anna."

The whole time, Anna just stood there, a slight smile on her face watching the two women talk.

"Look!" Dixie said, holding up one of Charlotte McLemore's books. Only this time she had turned it around to the back where the author's biography and picture were. Julie took the book from her hand and stared at the photo.

"Anna? Wait, I'm confused. You're Charlotte McLemore?"

Anna... or Charlotte, rather... smiled. "My real name is Anna, but my pen name is Charlotte."

Julie felt like she was going to throw up. Her insides were churning like some kind of alien was trying to escape. Certainly vomiting on the woman was probably not the right reaction given all of the terrible things she'd said about her book just yesterday.

"I'm so embarrassed," Julie said quietly.

"What's going on? What did I miss?" Dixie asked.

"Well, I met Anna yesterday, and I didn't know she was Charlotte... And I said some things about the book..."

Charlotte reached over and squeezed her shoulder. "It's no big deal, Julie. I really enjoyed it because nobody ever tells me the truth anymore. Everybody wants to say nice things, and that's great, but I also want to hear the bad things."

Julie looked up at her. "There are no bad things! I'm just a terrible reader. And I'm so tired lately. It wasn't your book!"

"It's fine, really. It was nice to talk to someone who had no idea who I was."

Dixie just continued staring at the situation in front of her. "I'm so sorry about this whole thing…"

"I am excited to be here, and I'm looking forward to spending the day with both of you while I sign books. And please, if you have constructive feedback about any of my books, I'd love to hear. I always want to become a better writer."

"You're a fabulous writer! Your books have been life-changing for me!" Dixie said, clasping her hands together like she was meeting God himself.

"Now, I see some muffins in that case over there, and I could sure use something on my stomach before we start this book signing. Mind if I grab one?"

"Honey, you can have as many muffins as your heart desires!" Dixie said, smiling.

CHAPTER 9

The book signing went off without a hitch, and Julie made an audible sigh of relief after the last customer left the shop. Charlotte spent the day signing her name, taking pictures with excited readers and chatting with each one like they were her best friend. Julie could see why people liked her and her books. She had such a way about her that made people feel comfortable.

"My hand feels like it just might fall off!" she said, rubbing the palm of her hand and then stretching her fingers back and forth. "But, I have to say I was shocked at how many readers came all the way to Seagrove."

"Me too!" Dixie said, pouring each of them a fresh cup of coffee. Even though it was almost lunch time, the coffee train never stopped at Down

Yonder. "I don't think we've ever had that many people in the store at one time."

"We definitely haven't," Julie interjected. "And I think we'd better order more Charlotte McLemore books!" She stood in front of the formerly full table and swiped her hand across.

"Thank you for having me here, ladies. This was so fun! Maybe we can do it again on my next release?"

Dixie nodded. "Of course!"

"Well, I think I'm going to head back to the inn and take a little nap."

"Don't you want some lunch?" Julie asked.

Charlotte touched her stomach. "I'm full of coffee and those delicious muffins, but I'll see you at dinner."

"Let me give you a ride," Dixie said, grabbing her purse.

"It's no bother. I can walk over the bridge."

"No, absolutely not!" Before Charlotte could say anything else, Dixie was holding the door open and pulling her keys out of her purse. There was no way Dixie was going to let her favorite author out of her sight when she could basically kidnap her for a few more minutes.

Julie watched as they disappeared down the side-walk. She leaned against the front counter and closed her eyes for a moment, taking a few deep breaths. There had been so many people in the store that it had almost become claustrophobic at times, and she wondered what it would be like to buy the space next door if it ever became available. Maybe they could expand and have even more to offer their customers. She'd even thought about having a whole cafe with trivia and karaoke nights, but she hadn't told Dixie her ideas just yet. None of it mattered if there wasn't a space to expand into anyway.

She turned and started wiping down the countertop. A germophobe, she constantly sanitized everything. She was cleaning out the coffee pot and refilling the water when she heard someone walk in the door behind her.

"Hey, Mom," Meg said.

"Oh, hey, honey! I didn't know you were coming by today."

Her daughter looked a little nervous, and that was never a good thing. As a mother, Julie never wanted to have difficult conversations with her daughters. She wanted everything to be all rainbows and unicorns, but life was rarely like that.

"I just dropped Vivi off with Christian. They're going to go down to the marsh to look at the birds."

"He's a good dad."

Meg smiled. "Yes, he is."

"And, he's going to be a wonderful husband. Which brings me to something I forgot to ask you yesterday. About the centerpieces…"

Meg held up her hand. "Mom, stop."

Julie was taken aback. "What do you mean?"

"Can we sit down?"

"Sure," Julie said, walking over and sitting down at the bistro table. Meg slowly joined her, not making eye contact. She placed both the palms of her hands on the table like she was trying to stabilize herself.

"I want to say that I am so thankful for all of the work that you've done on this wedding. I know it hasn't been easy, and you've been exhausted. I want to say that I'm sorry for putting so much responsibility on you."

"Oh, sweetie, I've enjoyed every minute of it! My daughter is getting married!"

"That's the thing…"

"What? You're not getting married?"

"No, I am getting married. But we've made a decision about something."

"What is it?"

"Mom, I've decided that I don't want a big wedding. All of this planning and trying to make this into some grand event just isn't me or Christian. We just want something really small with our family out by the ocean. That's it."

Julie stared at her for a long moment. When the shock finally wore off, she spoke. "Oh, thank God!"

Meg laughed. "What? I thought you'd be disappointed?"

"Are you kidding me? I felt like I was trying to plan a royal wedding. I'm so glad we're not doing that because it felt like it was way too much."

"Right? It started to feel like somebody else's event and not mine. I don't care about flowers and music and seating charts. I just want to marry Christian and get on with our lives."

Julie reached across the table and held her hands. "I am so glad that you're mature enough to know what's right for you and Christian. So we will do whatever you need us to do, but you make your wedding your own."

Meg smiled broadly and jumped up to hug her mother. "Thanks for understanding! All we need is to have our family there and maybe for grandma to make us a cake. Oh, and Lucy to make us some of her shrimp and grits!"

"You want shrimp and grits for your wedding meal?" Julie asked, laughing.

"Absolutely!"

"Then shrimp and grits you shall have!"

Janine stumbled, hanging onto William's arm for dear life. "At what point are you going to explain to me why I'm blindfolded?"

"We're almost there," he said, guiding her. She

could tell that they were on the beach, although she wasn't sure which one. The sand beneath her feet was thick, and she could feel her calves starting to burn.

When William had showed up at the yoga studio and asked her to go to lunch with him, this wasn't at all what she was expecting. He'd ushered her to his truck, put a blindfold on her and started driving. Wasn't this how a lot of scary movies started?

"How much further?"

He stopped. "We're here." He reached up and removed her blindfold, revealing a beautiful picnic lunch right by the water. They were at a little cove just down from Janine's cottage. She loved this area because it was quiet, although with the new light-house tours, there would probably be more people on that stretch of the beach very soon.

"You did this for me?"

"I just thought maybe you could use a little lunch away from all the craziness in the square right now." She had to admit, it was nice to get away from everything. With the Spring Festival starting tomorrow, there was a lot of activity going on around her studio.

"Thank you, William. This is a beautiful gesture."

He pointed to the red and white checkered blanket on the ground. She sat down cross legged, as any good Yogi would do.

"I picked up some of your favorites from the café. Chicken salad, potato soup, peach cobbler…"

Janine laughed. "Are you trying to make me fat?"

He smiled. "I'm just trying to make you happy, whatever that takes."

She reached over and held his hand. "I'm happy because I'm with you. I mean, I won't say no to the peach cobbler…"

"Janine, I'm really sorry for how things went the other night at the restaurant. I just had some things on my mind, and I pretty much ruined our romantic evening."

"Let's just forget about it and enjoy this amazing lunch, okay?"

"Yeah, and we better hurry up because I know you have a class in an hour or so."

"Yes, and I also have something else important I need to do after class this evening, so I might be a little late coming over to your house."

"I hope nothing too upsetting or dramatic?"

"I don't know. We'll see. I can't talk about it right now, but hopefully I can tell you when I see you tonight."

She didn't want to tell him about the situation with Emma without her permission first. She understood how important it was for a person who had suffered trauma to be able to control who knew about it.

"So, I wanted to talk to you about something…"

Her heart started to flutter. Maybe this was it. Maybe this was the moment that he was going to propose. Of course, she didn't know if that had been the plan at the restaurant, but maybe it was the plan now.

"Okay…"

"You and I have been together for a while now, and you know how much I love you and enjoy your company…"

"Excuse me! Excuse me!" A frantic woman came running from seemingly nowhere, waving her hands in the air.

"Oh good Lord…" William muttered under his breath.

"Is something wrong?" Janine said, standing up.

"Did you see a golden retriever run past here?"

"A golden retriever?" William said, irritation in his voice. Janine elbowed him.

"We're here visiting, and we saw this beautiful little stretch of beach. Thought we would come down here and check it out but my dog got off the leash. She doesn't know the area, and I'm scared to death she'll get eaten by an alligator or something worse!"

"What's worse than an alligator?" William muttered. This time, Janine pinched his arm.

The woman was obviously very upset, and Janine felt like they had to help her. "We haven't seen a dog, but we just got here. Maybe we can help you look for him."

William stared at her, surprise on his face. "Right. Of course we'll help. We weren't doing anything else," he said, dryly.

"We have to help her. She doesn't know the area," Janine whispered in his ear.

For the next thirty minutes, they scoured the beach, the trees nearby and even the backyards of the few cottages that were in that area. No sign of a dog. Finally, as they were all walking back to their cars, a very wet golden retriever came running up, barking, holding marsh grass in his mouth. Evidently, he had run far enough to end up in the marshlands, and he was probably pretty lucky that he didn't get eaten by an alligator.

"Elvis, are you crazy?" the woman yelled at her dog, as if he understood. Janine almost wanted to ask the backstory on naming her dog Elvis, but she was truly afraid the woman would spend the next half hour telling her, and she didn't have that kind of time. She had to get back to the studio and get ready for class. "Thank you so much for helping me look. I'm so sorry I interrupted your picnic."

"It's no problem, really. We're just glad you found your beloved Elvis," Janine said.

As they watched the woman walk off with her dog, William cleaned up the "picnic that never was". Janine grabbed a few bites of food, shoving them into her mouth quickly before they had to head back to town so she could teach class. She could tell that William was upset, but she wasn't totally sure why. Even though she was assuming that he was yet again going to try to propose, she was starting to feel like something was always going to get in their way.

Being the woo-woo type of person that she was, that was starting to concern her. Maybe the universe was putting obstacles in their path so that they didn't end up married. And maybe he wasn't going to ask her at all. Maybe she was just pie-in-the-sky dreaming things up in her head. At this point, she didn't know what to think.

"Well, thanks for the picnic," she said, forcing a smile.

"There was no picnic. Instead, there was a search for an idiot dog named Elvis who likes to eat marsh grass."

She smiled. "It's okay, William. We have plenty of time for picnics. At least we did a good deed today."

"I guess so. Good luck with your class. I'll see you tonight."

She hopped out of the truck and watched him drive away wondering whether they would ever get married or if she was destined to just be his girlfriend for the rest of her life.

E mma locked the door to the lighthouse after the last guest left. Today had been a long one with two school groups, a church group and a screaming baby that seemed to echo through the entire building.

All she wanted to do was run herself a bubble bath in the old clawfoot tub that was in the cottage and soak until her skin turned into a prune-like texture.

This morning, she had gotten a call from Caroline who had, of course, talked to Steve. Again, she tried to talk some sense into Emma, but Emma couldn't seem to make her understand that she wasn't coming home. This was her new home, and she was starting to find some semblance of happiness here.

The ocean soothed her. The marshes still scared her a little bit, but she was starting to grow accustomed to the smells and the sounds that happened at night in the South Carolina lowcountry.

She was looking forward to manning her own table at the Spring Festival tomorrow. She had worked up the flyers which the city council had approved, and she was hoping to bring even more business to the lighthouse. As long as she did a good job with the tours, she got to keep her job. She got to keep her free housing. She got to continue living her new life.

"Hey!"

She turned around to see Janine standing near her front door. She wasn't expecting company, and normally she wouldn't have minded if she wasn't so incredibly tired.

"Hey, Janine. I didn't know you were coming by this evening."

"I know, and it's really rude of me to just show up here but I need to talk to you."

"Did something else happen with William?"

"Well… Yes."

"Then by all means, come on in. I was about to heat up some spaghetti I made last night. Hungry?"

"Actually, yes I am hungry. I didn't exactly get to eat lunch today."

"No? Why is that?"

She put the key in the door and allowed Janine inside. She pointed at the breakfast bar for Janine to sit down as she went to the refrigerator to retrieve the spaghetti and the now too soggy garlic bread. Maybe if she threw it in the toaster, she could get it to crisp up again.

"So, William took me for a romantic picnic by the ocean today."

"Wow. He's Mr. Romance lately. So why didn't you eat lunch then? Too much romance going on?" Emma said, winking.

"No. A tourist came running through saying that her dog was missing, so I felt like we needed to spend the time to help her. Ended up barely making it back in time to teach my class and only having a few bites of food for lunch."

"I imagine William was not happy about that?"

"You imagine right. I got the feeling that he might be popping the question again. But I could be totally wrong and overthinking this. Maybe he's just trying to do something romantic, but he's not actually going to ask me."

"Have you ever thought about flipping the tables and asking him instead?"

Janine pondered that for a moment. "I've thought about it, but I guess I'm too traditionally southern. I just feel like the man should ask."

"I have to agree with you there. Some things are just set in stone for me."

"Listen, I didn't actually come here to talk to you about William and me."

Emma finished doling the spaghetti out onto plates and put them into the microwave to heat up. Then, she popped the garlic bread into the toaster.

"Oh yeah? What's up?"

"I don't know how to say this exactly… I've been trying to figure it out the whole time I was waiting for you to come out of the lighthouse."

"Now you're starting to scare me a little bit."

"Emma, *I know*."

"You know what?"

"I know what happened."

"Janine, you're gonna have to be a little more specific. You know what happened? What does that mean?"

Janine blew out a long breath. "I know that you were a police officer and that you were in an officer involved shooting."

Emma was holding the dirty serving spoon in her hand, covered with tomato sauce. She immediately dropped it, causing a loud clanging sound on the tile floor in the kitchen. It felt like all of the blood had drained from her face, and there was a really distinct possibility that she might just pass out. She had only done that once in her life, so she knew exactly what it felt like. So she braced herself against the counter, her hands gripping the granite. She could see the blood leaving her fingers as they looked white from holding onto the countertop so hard.

"Are you okay?" Janine said, immediately realizing something was wrong. She jumped up and put her arm around Emma's waist. "Why don't we sit down?"

They walked over to the dining table and Emma slowly slid down into one of the chairs. She had figured at some point someone would know who she was, but this wasn't the reaction she expected from herself. She had been in so many adrenaline inducing situations in her career that she should've been able to handle any kind of stress, but right now she felt like she could be knocked over with a feather.

"How did you find out?" she asked, softly.

"Colleen saw it on a true crime documentary last night. She came and told me, but she hasn't told anyone else and she won't. We are the only two people who know."

"Oh my gosh. I can't get away from it! It's on a documentary? Why can't I get away from this?"

She stood up and started pacing back-and-forth in the kitchen like a wild animal.

"Why don't you sit back down? I don't think you should be…"

"Do you know what it was like? How hard it was to stay in that town after it happened? Everybody looked at me differently. Everybody judged me."

"I'm sure that wasn't true, Emma. You did the right thing. It sounds like he would've killed you or someone else if you hadn't done what you did."

"I could've shot him in the leg or tackled him or done literally anything else…"

"You can't second-guess yourself! I know police officers, and I know what kind of training you go through. You have to make split-second decisions that the rest of us can't even imagine. And it's just the luck of the draw who ends up having to make those decisions in the field. You did the right thing. Otherwise you would've been in trouble or lost your job, but everybody knows that you protected yourself and your community."

She sat down and put her head in her hands. "I thought I could start over here, but this is going to follow me forever. I'll always be known as the cop who killed somebody."

"A lot of cops are in that club, unfortunately. It's part of the job."

"You know, I never really wanted to be a police officer. I was running from something then and I ran straight into that. And if I hadn't made the decision to become an officer, I wouldn't be feeling like this right now."

"Emma, I can't pretend to understand what you're going through, but have you gotten any counseling?"

She laughed under her breath. "What counselor is going to understand what I'm going through?"

"I don't think it's about someone understanding what you're going through. I think it's about helping you learn how to accept what you've gone through and forgive yourself."

She sat there for a moment quietly thinking about what Janine had said. She couldn't keep going on like this, that much was for sure. It was exhausting trying to hide who she was all the time. She felt like she was living a double life, constantly trying to pretend she was okay. She'd been involved in a case where a person was put into witness protection, and she often wondered what that life was like. Now, she had at least a small taste of it.

"When I was a kid, I used to save bugs. I drove my mother crazy because I was constantly bringing them into the house in Mason jars or her good Tupperware. But I didn't want them to die. And if I stepped on one accidentally, I would cry. I couldn't imagine hurting another living creature."

"I was kind of that way too," Janine said, smiling. "We're tender hearted people, I guess."

"So, when I was a police officer, I prided myself on taking care of the people of my community. Even the ones who did wrong, I treated with respect. I tried to never hurt anybody. Of course, I had to tackle people or handcuff them. That came with the job, but I always did it in the most respectful way I could no matter who they were or what they did."

"I believe that about you."

She could feel tears starting to roll down her cheeks. "And then there was that night. It was dark in the building, and the negotiators were outside trying to get him to give himself up. He just wouldn't do it. In the back of my mind, I knew how many women he had raped, and I knew we couldn't let him get out of there."

"You don't have to talk about this, Emma."

"I walked down the dark hallway all by myself. I went in without any back up because I thought since I am small and pretty stealth, I could get in there.

And I came around the corner, my gun drawn, and I was face-to-face with him. He had a gun on me, and I had a gun on him, and he had a hostage around in front of him in a chokehold.

"Oh my gosh…"

"It seemed like it lasted several minutes, but it was really only a few seconds. He yelled at me to drop the gun, and I yelled at him to drop his gun. And I could just see the look on that woman's face. She was terrified. I knew he was crazy enough to just shoot her and me. And so I made a split second decision that I can't take back. He obviously deserved to go to jail for the rest of his life, but I am the person who didn't even want to step on a bug, and now I've taken a human life. I can't take that back. It's just permanently stuck there in my brain."

"But you saved a human life. You saved that woman, Emma. And now she can live the rest of her life doing good things in the community. I'm sure she has a family that is very grateful for what you did that night."

"I know logically that I did the right thing. My bosses all told me that I did the right thing. I even got a commendation for heroism, but I see his face. I see him laying on the ground when I go to sleep at night. I see what nobody else had to see, and I just can't get it out of my mind. I wake up every night drenched in sweat, heart pounding. My own screaming wakes me up sometimes."

Janine stood up walked over and hugged Emma around the neck. Emma leaned her head over onto Janine's shoulder and just cried. She hadn't cried since the night of the shooting. She'd kept it all inside, pushing it down until it was almost like a can of soda that someone had shaken up.

"I know what it's like to have trauma, and I also know that you have to talk this out in a way that helps you get past it and forgive yourself. I would like for you to come to a support group with me. Even if you're not ready to talk to a counselor yet, my support group for trauma survivors is wonderful."

"I don't know…"

"Emma, let this new start be a *real* new start. Don't let it just be the place you're running to in order to get away from what happened. Let people support you. These people understand. I promise."

Finally, Emma felt a weight lifted off of her shoulders. She felt lighter just knowing that someone else knew her secret. The burden wasn't hers alone to carry now.

"Do you feel differently about me now that you know?"

Janine shook her head. "Absolutely not. I feel like we're sisters. We've both suffered trauma, and we're both survivors. And I'm thriving now. You're going to be thriving soon too. Just take my hand and let me help you."

Emma looked down at Janine holding out her hand. Was it time for her to finally get past this? Was it time for her to open up and let other people in? She reached out and took Janine's hand.

"Okay."

"Okay?" Janine said, smiling as tears rolled down her face too. She hugged Emma even tighter. "We're going to do this together."

CHAPTER 10

*J*ulie was up bright and early ready for the spring festival. It was one of her favorite parts of the year because it meant that the warmer weather was being ushered in along with all of the tourists who would not only bring more money to the bookstore but also to the inn. Both of her businesses relied heavily on welcoming people to Seagrove.

The spring festival brought in tourists from all over the area, but also all of the locals. It was so great to see everyone in one place and take the time to relax and catch up on all of the town's gossip. She had been sitting at the table for Down Yonder Books for the last couple of hours, handing out free book-marks and discount coupons.

"It's a beautiful day, isn't it?" her mother, SuAnn, asked as she walked up to the table. She picked up one of the bookmarks, looked at it and then scrunched her nose before setting it back down on the table. "Do people actually like those?"

"Yes, Mom. People like them. So how's everything going at your table?"

SuAnn had quite a spread at her table with pound cakes, cupcakes and even German chocolate cake. She had been on a baking frenzy trying to get ready for the festival, and she was selling a lot from what Julie could tell from across the square.

"We can't keep up with the pace! Darcy is sitting at the table now, and I think we're almost out of peach pound cake. You know that's everybody's favorite."

"Sounds like you better get back in the store and start baking."

"Lord no! I was up until all kinds of ungodly hours last night baking. I'm done! If they want more, they can come to the store and buy it on Monday."

"Mom, I want you to meet Charlotte McLemore."

SuAnn smiled. "It's truly an honor to meet you, Charlotte. I just love your books! The Magnolia Mystery series kept me up reading so much one night that I overslept the next morning. Good thing I own the place!" She slapped the table and laughed at her own joke.

"Well, thank you very much. It's always so nice to meet my readers," Charlotte said.

"And I heard my daughter here stuck her foot in

her mouth before she knew who you were?" SuAnn looked at Julie and rolled her eyes.

"She just told the truth. Not everybody is going to like my books, just like I'm sure not everybody likes your baked goods."

SuAnn stared at her. "Honey, I haven't found anybody who hasn't liked my cakes."

"Down, mother." Julie said.

"I didn't mean to offend," Charlotte said. She cut her eyes at Julie and smiled slyly. Julie liked Charlotte more and more the longer she knew her.

As SuAnn wandered off to probably harass somebody else, she looked over at Charlotte. "Sorry about her. We try to keep her corralled as much as possible, but she's got a sharp tongue and no filter between her brain and mouth."

"My mother is the same way. I love her to death, but I try not to take her out in public."

Julie laughed. "And again, I hope you didn't take any offense to what I said about your book. It was truly exhaustion speaking. Now that I don't have to worry about my daughter's wedding situation, I'm going to sit down and read that book every night until I finish it."

Charlotte squeezed her arm. "Don't do that. Use your life for stuff you enjoy, not for stuff you dread. Not everybody likes to read, and not everybody likes to read my books."

"For somebody who has such a huge fan base, you sure do seem to take everything in stride."

Charlotte shrugged her shoulders. " You kind of have to when you've been through what I've been through."

Julie cocked her head. "What you've been through?"

"You don't know? I am a two-time cancer survivor. The last time was just a couple of years ago right before I wrote that book that you have been trying to read."

Julie had had no idea."Really? That's amazing that you're such a survivor." She really did admire Charlotte even more now. Strong southern women were the people she most admired in the world, and she was thankful to be surrounded by them most of the time.

A reader walked up to the table and Charlotte stopped to take a picture with her and sign a book. She then turned back to Julie. "I learned during that time that I can't let little things get to me. I just have to live my life in the best, biggest way that I know how."

"That's very true. After all, we only get one life!"

"Some of us don't believe that," Janine said, walking up to the table.

"What are you talking about, sis?"

"Well, some people believe that we reincarnate over and over and live many lives. And the things that we go through here on earth might be because of things we didn't learn in a past life."

Julie rolled her eyes. "Charlotte, this is my sister, Janine. She's a little woo-woo but we love her anyway."

Janine slapped her on the shoulder. "Nice to meet you, Charlotte. I've heard wonderful things about your books."

"Thank you."

"I just came by to let you know that William is going to be in the boat parade later."

"Oh yeah? Like the one we did at Christmas?"

"Very similar, I think. We will all gather along the marsh and the docks, and different boats will float by and throw candy and generally have a good time while we watch them pass."

"That sounds fun. I grew up on boats, so I'd like to be a part of that if you all walk over there," Charlotte said with a smile.

"Of course! We'll head over as soon as we're finished here."

As Janine walked off, Julie looked around the square. She saw Dixie walking hand-in-hand with Harry, looking at different tables and picking up crafts people were selling. She saw Colleen and Tucker giggling under the tree like a couple of madly in love school children. Every so often, Tucker would feed Colleen a bite of ice cream and then they would laugh all over again.

And of course, she saw Meg and Christian with Vivi over by the face painting station. Vivi was getting a butterfly painted on her cheek, although she was squirming so much that there was no telling what it was going to look like when the poor volunteer was finished doing it.

And then there was Emma who was sitting at a table, handing out flyers and other information about the lighthouse. She seemed a little down today, but she was still doing her job and would occasionally smile and wave from across the way.

Julie truly loved her community. There wasn't anything she wouldn't do for the people who had supported her and made her a part of them. When she had shown up in Seagrove, so broken and lost, she never imagined that these people would literally just fold her into their lives like she had always been there. She was no longer the newcomer. She was a full-fledged Seagrove resident and proud of it.

"You know, I've been working on a novel for over a year now. I'm sure authors hate when people tell them that, but since I think we're sort of friends now…"

Charlotte smiled broadly. "I love to hear when people are writing books. The more creativity we have out in the world, the better. What's it about?"

"Oh, I won't bore you with it."

"I want to know!"

Julie spent the next few minutes explaining the

plot and her ideas for the rest of the book. Surprisingly, Charlotte sat and listened the whole time. Of course, she was probably just being nice, but Julie appreciated it all the same.

"You know, Julie, you've got a great idea there. I'd love to read a few pages if you don't mind?"

"Really?"

"Sure!"

"I would be so honored if you would. Thank you, Charlotte."

"I'll take a look when we get back to the inn later. Will that work?"

"Of course!"

Emma sat behind the table trying her best to look happy as she greeted people that wanted to know more about the lighthouse. In reality, she was still very emotional after her conversation with Janine the night before.

Janine had apologized over and over for bringing it up when Emma had such a big day planned for the spring festival. But she told Janine that she was glad to finally have it out in the open. Not that she wanted everyone in town to know who she was, but Janine was her best friend in Seagrove right now, and she trusted her.

They had talked late into the night even after

eating dinner. Janine shared more of her story, and Emma was glad to know that she wasn't alone. She also felt much better about the details of what had happened, and she felt like she was already beating herself up less and less. Still, she struggled with the decision she'd been forced to make, and she wasn't totally confident that a support group or a counselor would be able to help her come to terms with that.

After Janine left, she actually sent Steve a message apologizing for the way she reacted when he came to the cottage. She told him that she had loved him, but that she just wasn't going to be the same person. She was going to be a better person, but she simply could not see herself with the life he wanted. She didn't want to be in the security business, she didn't want to work long enough to retire from the force. And she certainly didn't want to be married to a police officer. It was something she didn't want in her life anymore.

She had great respect for law-enforcement, and she always would. But being married to someone who came home every night dressed in uniform with stories about their day was just going to further traumatize her. He said he understood, and she felt like they finally cleared the air.

She had called Caroline and tried to explain what she was doing.

"You know I can refer you to someone, right?" *Caroline had said, concern filling her voice.*

"I know, and I appreciate that. But, I have to do what feels right for me. Taking baby steps is what feels appropriate right now."

"And you're sure you're not moving back home?"

Emma laughed. "This is my home now. One day, I'll invite you for a visit, and you'll see why I love it. I'm okay, Caroline. I promise."

Being a licensed clinical social worker, Caroline had been very concerned about her best friend, but when they hung up, Emma felt like she had proven to her that she was going to get the right kind of help now.

Janine told her all about the trauma support group that she sometimes attended, and it had really helped her. Janine seemed so put together now, so it was hard for Emma to picture her when she was in the midst of trying to recover from what happened to her.

This morning, she was just feeling all rung out, like she needed a very long nap followed by a big tub of ice cream. She didn't get the chance to really rest after her conversations, and she was looking forward to a very quiet night at home after the festival.

"How's everything going?" Janine asked. She had been flitting about, here and there, showing people different yoga poses and inviting them to classes. Emma loved to watch her work. She couldn't believe how incredibly flexible she was, and everybody in town seemed to know Janine. With her head full of thick, curly hair, it was hard to miss her.

"Really good. I've met a lot of nice people, and I have recited every single lighthouse fact that I know."

Janine chuckled. "I'm sure you're feeling a little worn out today? This will all be over soon, and we can go watch the boat parade."

"Boat parade? You mean there's more?" Emma wanted to lay her head on the table and cry quietly.

"Don't worry, it doesn't last long. But I have to go support William because he's in it. It's good for business."

"Then I'll be there. I wouldn't want William to think I'm not a team player."

Janine laughed. "Well, I better go grab some more flyers. Got to fill up those yoga classes!" she said as she trotted off.

Emma was so happy to have found a place like Seagrove. She felt like she'd won the lottery. Were there other towns like this across the United States that nobody talked about but were perfect little pieces of heaven? She almost didn't want to tell anyone where she lived for fear that everyone would want to move there. She imagined that there was a delicate balance in a town like this, and she hoped that it never ended up on one of those lists in a magazine saying it was America's best small town.

There was nothing more beautiful than seeing the sunset over the lowcountry marshes. As William stared out over the marsh grass that was slightly blowing in the wind, he thought about how many years of his life he'd spent in this water. Fishing, boating, and occasionally falling in and swimming back to the boat. So many good memories as a kid, and so many new memories that he got to make every day.

As he floated along, he stood up and started waving to the crowds that were forming on shore. Up ahead, he would surely see his mom, Janine and the rest of the crew.

He was thankful to have all of their support even when he had made such rash decisions like opening the boat charter service. Everybody had supported him, and that was just how they were. Supportive. He didn't surround himself with anyone who made him feel like his dreams were stupid, least of all Janine.

She supported everything he did, every idea he had, even the stupid ones. And he just felt terrible that the two times he had tried to propose to her, something had happened to interrupt them. She must think that he's crazy by now.

He could see her up ahead, her curly hair blowing in the breeze. As usual, she was smiling and clapping and waving, her perky personality always coming through. And in that moment, he was filled with such gratitude and love that it was almost overwhelming. He could feel tears welling in his eyes as he looked at her off in the distance.

And that's when he realized what he had to do. There was no more waiting, no more orchestrated romantic moments. Life was about those spontaneous moments, the ones that became memories that stayed with you forever.

So as the boat came closer to the dock where Janine and everyone she knew was standing, he cut the motor to his boat so that he could slow down.

"There's my man!" Janine yelled, waving and blowing kisses at him. And as he came closer up to the dock, he went down on one knee and called to her.

"Janine, will you marry me?" he yelled as loud as he could. He held up the little black box that had stayed in his pocket since the first night he tried to propose. Janine stood there, stunned, her eyes wide.

"Are you serious?" she called back.

He grabbed the rope on the side of the boat and threw it as hard as he could so that Dawson could pull him closer to the dock. Thank goodness his friend was standing so close and was able to catch it. Dawson pulled and pulled until the boat banged into the side of the dock, shaking everyone who was standing there.

It wasn't the most seamless proposal, but it sure would be memorable. As the boat came to a stop, he looked up at her. She was covering her face, except for her eyes, tears welling in them.

"Yes, I'm serious. Janine, will you please do me the honor of becoming my wife?"

She screamed yes and started jumping up and down, shaking the dock again. All of the people standing on it were probably worried they were going to fall straight into the water at any moment.

William jumped off the boat, swept her up in his arms and twirled her around. When he finally put her down, he slipped the ring on her finger and the crowd went wild. There were very few dry eyes standing on that dock, but there were plenty of applause and cheers to go around.

He took Janine's hand and helped her into the boat. "I think my future wife should finish the boat parade with me," he said, smiling.

"Your future wife will go anywhere you want to go," she said, putting her arm around him as he turned on the motor and started back through the waters of the marsh.

As they pulled away from the crowd of people, William took the boat out into more open water and stopped it again. "Well, were you surprised?"

Janine smiled as she looked down at her ring. "Absolutely!"

"Come on now. You had to know I was trying to propose over and over lately."

She bit her lip. "Okay, maybe I thought you were going to propose, but I wasn't sure."

He pulled her into a tight hug. "Thank you for saying yes."

She looked up at him. "Seriously? Why wouldn't I say yes?"

"Because you're beautiful Janine, and I'm just regular old William. I'm marrying up. You know that, right?"

Janine giggled. "Let's see if you say that after five years of living with me!"

"I will cherish being married to you until the end of my days, Janine. And I'm so grateful this whole proposal thing is finally over!"

"Me too! No more competing couples and wet dogs!"

"So, when should we get hitched?"

She thought for a moment, putting her finger on her chin. "I've always wanted a fall wedding."

"Then we'll get married this fall!"

She grinned broader than he'd ever seen her grin. "I can't wait to marry you."

"Ditto," he said before dipping her downward to give her a kiss.

CHAPTER 11

*E*mma was very nervous. She was second-guessing herself over and over again, wondering why she had made such a rash decision. But, in an effort to start healing her trauma, she had reached out to the woman whose life she had saved that night.

The woman and her family had tried getting in touch with Emma several times, but each time she ignored them. She just couldn't face seeing the woman again. She hadn't wanted to hear words about being a hero, but she was ready now to face her.

Of course, it would be done through video chat since the woman lived in Nashville and Emma was in Seagrove, but it was still nerve-racking just the same.

Janine had offered to come to her house and sit

with her, but it was something that she thought she really should do alone. She didn't know how she would react to seeing Ellen again. She often saw her fearful face in her dreams, and she was a little worried that she would have a PTSD moment as soon as the camera switched on.

The last time she saw Ellen was in that dark building, the light on her gun shining on her face. When the whole thing was over, Emma was rushed to the station for debriefing, and everything after that was a complete blur to her. Much of that time in her life had been blocked out by her brain in an effort to protect her mental health.

She rubbed her hands together and then rubbed them on the front of her shorts. It was a nervous habit she used to do before tests back in her school days. She hadn't exactly been the best student, often wanting to do something more artistic than math. She had barely made it out of school by the skin of her teeth, but when she walked at graduation she had been so proud of herself for getting it done.

College had never been in the cards for her, and that was another reason that she ended up going through the police academy instead. No math required. Just a willingness to be full of adrenaline for hours each day and put her life on the line regularly. Still better than math was her opinion back then. Turned out, running a lighthouse also didn't require a lot of math skills. Sometimes she had the urge to call her old algebra teacher and brag about how she was right that she'd never need to know that stuff.

When she heard her phone start to ring, she almost wanted to run straight out the door of the cottage. Why was she doing this? She wasn't ready. She should text the woman and tell her she changed her mind. So many things were bouncing around inside of her head. But right now, she just had to be brave. Just in this moment. Just for the next few minutes. She had certainly been through worse.

She pressed the green button on the front of her phone and a second later, there was Ellen on the other side, smiling. She wasn't fearful, she wasn't crying. She was smiling, and that immediately calmed some of Emma's nerves.

"Hi, Emma! I'm so glad you agreed to talk to me!"

Emma forced a smile so that she didn't look like some kind of crazy person sitting there with a deer in the headlights look. "Hi, Ellen. It's so nice to see you under such different circumstances."

Ellen nodded. "Very true. The last time you saw me must've been very traumatizing for you. I just remember being terrified, and then I saw you and I wasn't so scared anymore because I could tell you were going to handle the situation. And you did."

Emma swallowed hard. "So, how are you now?"

She took in a breath and blew it out. "I have good days and bad days. Some days I just survive, but it's getting better each day. I've been seeing a therapist since right after the incident, and that has helped me a lot."

"That's good. I'm glad that you are getting better."

"They tell me I have PTSD, and for the first few weeks after the shooting, I was having nearly constant panic attacks and nightmares when I would go to sleep. Even a car backfiring would set me off."

"I understand, trust me."

"That was another reason why I wanted to talk to you. I feel like you have to be so affected by this whole thing too, and I wanted to make sure that you're okay. Are you getting some help?"

"Honestly, I was very resistant to that idea until recently. But I have moved to a different town, and I'm out of the police force so I think I'm ready now to start seeing someone. Like you, I get the nightmares."

"Just know that it does get better. You have to work at it, but it will progressively improve. At least that's how it has worked for me."

"Well, thank you for talking to me. I can't explain it, but I just needed to know that you were okay."

"My brother is a firefighter, and he has saved some people over the years. I know that he doesn't like being called a hero. It makes him feel uncomfortable. And I feel like maybe you're uncomfortable with being called a hero because of the situation. I just want you to know that saving my life wasn't in vain. Not only did you keep me from being attacked by that vicious creature, but you've allowed me to have extra time with my husband and kids. And I'm going back to school to become a nurse!"

"Wow! That's fantastic! I'm so glad you're moving forward."

"It's all thanks to you. But if you don't want to be called a hero, I just want you to know that what you did mattered. And while a life was lost in that process, just remember that he chose that. You didn't."

As they said their goodbyes, Emma thought about her last statement over and over. That the guy - whose name happened to be Ricky - chose what happened to him. She had never thought about it that way. This whole time she'd been putting the blame on herself, but maybe that was wrong. Maybe his actions foretold his destiny. She just happened to be the conduit that connected his actions to his outcome.

He chose to attack women. He chose to take one hostage. He chose to point a gun at a police officer. His choices led her to have to make the most diffi-cult one of her life. She didn't choose to kill another human being. She was forced to make a choice between his life and the life of an innocent woman, and she made the *only* decision.

~

J ulie and Charlotte laid on their chaise lounges on the beach, the wind blowing toward them as they each drank a cup of coffee. The spring festival had been exhausting, and Julie was glad it was over even though she had enjoyed it immensely.

Seeing her sister and William get engaged in such a romantic and spontaneous way made her giddy with delight. She couldn't wait to see them finally get married and start their lives together. Janine had talked a lot about adoption, and she was thrilled at the idea of finally getting a niece or nephew.

"Lucy makes a dang good cup of coffee," Charlotte said.

"She certainly does. And those pancakes this morning? The woman knows her way around the kitchen, doesn't she?"

"Yes, she does," Charlotte said, setting her book on the table between them and sighing. "I almost hate to leave here. You live in heaven on earth, Julie."

"Well, don't tell anybody. We certainly don't want thousands of extra people moving here and messing up our balance."

Charlotte laughed. "My lips are sealed. Listen, I wanted to talk to you about your book."

Julie cringed. How she wished she hadn't handed Charlotte those few pages of her work in progress last night. But she was feeling excited after the festival and the proposal, and she just wasn't thinking straight. It was in no way her best work, and it hadn't even been edited yet.

"Listen, I know it isn't good. I've never written anything like that before…"

"No, it's fabulous!"

Julie looked at her. "Charlotte, you don't have to try to be nice. I understand that writing is a lot harder than it looks."

"Not if you have natural talent, and I think you do. So, I wanted to ask your permission to send this over to my publisher. Just let some of my contacts take a look and see if they think there's marketability there."

Julie was in shock. "What? Are you serious? You want to send that to your publisher?"

"I think it's worth a shot. There aren't a lot of great books for women in this age group, and I don't mind a little extra competition."

"I don't think I'm going to be any competition for you," Julie said, laughing. "But feel free to give it to your publisher. They might need a good laugh."

"Don't sell yourself short. I didn't think I would have the success that I have, but here I am!"

"So when do you have to leave?"

"Tomorrow morning. I have a book signing tomorrow evening in Savannah. So I need to make the drive and go to my hotel."

"I'm really going to miss you around here. It was nice having somebody to talk to."

"Oh, I'll be in touch. I'm sure my publishers are probably going to want to talk to you."

Julie crossed her fingers. "We can only hope!"

"And, truth be told, I'd like to have a second home here in Seagrove someday. I feel at home here."

"We'd love to have you! Although, I'd lock your doors because I'm afraid Dixie might try to break in and have dinner with you," Julie said with a laugh.

Dixie locked up the bookstore and turned to walk down the sidewalk to her car. She was exhausted after the festival, but she'd had to come back to the store to retrieve her tote bag and empty the coffee pot.

"Hey, old lady!" She turned around to see SuAnn doing the same thing. She was locking the door to her bakery.

"Old lady? You're one to talk!" Dixie replied, laughing.

They met in the middle between their two stores. Over the last few months, they had managed to forge a strange friendship that mainly consisted of sarcastic comments and the occasional sit down coffee date to gossip about everyone they knew.

"So how did the festival go for you?" SuAnn asked.

"Pretty good. Julie handled most of it so I could

walk around with Harry. He's still having some back trouble, so we couldn't do a whole lot."

"We sold out of all of our cakes. I think I will have a bunch of new customers on Monday morning!"

"That's great! Where is Nick?"

"Oh, he had to go out of town to visit his niece. She just had a baby."

"How nice. He seems like a lovely man."

"He is. The love of my life," SuAnn said, smiling. It wasn't often that a person could get SuAnn to open up and act like a normal human being, but Nick seemed to have a special touch.

"So where are you headed?"

"I guess I'm going to go home and rest these old feet. Maybe take a bubble bath and drink several glasses of wine."

"Well, I don't drink the wine because I can't mix it with my medication, but I think a nice bath sounds like a wonderful idea."

"Say, Dixie, do you ever feel like we are the luck-iest women in the world?"

Dixie tilted her head to the side. "What do you mean?"

"I mean we're still vital at our ages, still building successful businesses. We have wonderful men in our lives, great kids. I even have a great-grand-daughter now. And William and Janine just got engaged. We live in this fantastic little town. Sometimes it just seems like we have been given way more blessings than we might deserve." It wasn't often that SuAnn spoke so poetically.

Dixie thought for a moment. "We are blessed beyond measure."

"We sure are. Well, I guess I better get home. Nick is supposed to be calling me in a little bit."

"Have a good night, SuAnn. I'll see you back here on Monday."

"Enjoy your bath," SuAnn said, laughing as she turned around and walked towards her car.

The Fourth of July had always been one of Julie's favorite holidays. Aside from the patriotism of it all, she loved the fireworks, a cookout and the gathering of family and friends. And this Fourth of July, they had so many different things to celebrate.

Having a party at the inn had become one of her favorite traditions. Lucy and Dawson had spent the whole afternoon cooking up all kinds of food, with Lucy in the kitchen and Dawson on the grill. They had invited several people from town including their family and friends.

Meg and Christian had gotten married in May, and it had been a small affair right there on the beach like Meg had wanted. It turned out to be the perfect little wedding, and Vivi looked adorable as the flower girl being pulled in a wagon by Dylan.

And then there was Emma, the new resident in town. She had become a constant fixture in their social scene. She and Janine were very good friends, and she was settling in to Seagrove like she had always been there.

Emma had confided in Julie about her past, and she had talked to Colleen as well since she was the one who had figured out who Emma was. Nobody thought any less of her, and they all understood the situation she found herself in as a police officer. Eventually, Emma started to forgive herself.

She had been going to support group meetings with Janine for a long time and recently had started to see a trauma counselor. It was helping her so much, and she was smiling more and more. She seemed at peace, like she had forgiven herself for taking someone's life. There was some level of PTSD she was still dealing with, but she was determined to fight it with everything she had through counseling and the support of others.

Seagrove was a place where a lot of people came to recover from whatever life had thrown at them, including Julie. It was like a hospital for hearts. The ocean, the people and just the sense of community did a lot to soothe people who had gone through sometimes horrible things.

"How did you like those ribs?" Dawson asked, walking up behind her and sliding his arms around her waist. She loved when he did that. It made her feel safe and secure.

"Fabulous, as always," she said, looking up at him. He gave her a quick peck on the lips.

"I feel like our get togethers are getting larger and larger with each holiday."

She smiled. "Isn't that great? I just love that we have so many family and friends, and I also love that we have this great big property to host them."

"I do too. It's a dream come true. You know, I lived a very lonely life here for a long time before I met you."

She turned around and looked up at him, rubbing her thumb across his five o'clock shadow. "So, are you saying you were lost before you met me, Dawson Lancaster?"

"I would say that's pretty true."

"I was being sarcastic."

"And I was being serious," he said, pinching her cheek.

"Can you believe that William and Janine are engaged?" she said, as she turned back around and noticed them standing over by the picnic table.

"I think we all knew it would happen eventually. William is just a slow poke."

"Still, it was a pretty romantic proposal."

"That it was."

They stood there quietly watching all of their friends and family, and Julie smiled the whole time.

She saw Dixie slow dancing with her husband. She saw her own mother playing with Julie's new son. She saw Colleen and Tucker running while holding hands with Vivi and swinging her up into the air.

There were so many things to be thankful for in her life, and she couldn't wait to see what the future would bring. If it was anything like the present, it was going to be a perfectly wild ride.

Visit www.RachelHannaAuthor.com for a list of all of Rachel's books!

Made in the USA
Columbia, SC
07 June 2022

61472938R00105